THE BAY

DARNELL BAYNES . . . As a young man, he took a bullet to win his wife. Now his sons are grown and he's taught them the lessons he learned in life: Pay your debts. .y your prayers. And never forget that being right doesn't matter much if you're slow on the draw . . .

LUKE BAYNES . . . Darnell's firstborn son, Luke, didn't talk much if he didn't have to. But when he did, it was worth listening to . . .

MILT BAYNES . . . Proud and quick with a joke, he could move through the woods as fast and quiet as a buzzard's shadow. And he was always ready for a fight . . .

WARD BAYNES . . . The youngest of the Baynes boys, he had to grow up fast. But as his pa once said, he had an advantage—because no one expects the youngest cub to be the most dangerous . . .

ROD SILVANA . . . Darnell Baynes's nephew wore fancy clothes, spoke several languages, and didn't seem that tough. But underneath it all, he could fight like a Baynes . . .

THE BAYNES CLAN

KANSAS GAMBLER

JOHN S. McCORD

B

BERKLEY BOOKS, NEW YORK

All of the characters in this book, except for certain historical figures, are fictitious, and any resemblance to actual persons, living or dead, is purely coincidental.

THE BAYNES CLAN: KANSAS GAMBLER

A Berkley Book / published by arrangement with the author

PRINTING HISTORY
Berkley edition / September 1997

All rights reserved.
Copyright © 1997 by John S. McCord.
This book may not be reproduced in whole or in part, by mimeograph or any other means, without permission. For information address: The Berkley Publishing Group, a member of Penguin Putnam Inc., 200 Madison Avenue, New York, New York 10016.

The Putnam Berkley World Wide Web site address is http://www.berkley.com

ISBN: 0-425-15719-9

BERKLEY®
Berkley Books are published by The Berkley Publishing Group, a member of Penguin Putnam Inc., 200 Madison Avenue, New York, New York 10016. BERKLEY and the "B" design are trademarks belonging to Berkley Publishing Corporation.

PRINTED IN THE UNITED STATES OF AMERICA

10 9 8 7 6 5 4 3 2 1

ONE

SOMEONE HAD MANAGED to switch decks. Rod
Silvana's first card, a trifle bit cooler than it should have
been, signaled the introduction of a "cold" deck. It
lacked the slight warmth from handling that cards pick
up during play. Rod's irritation at having missed the
exchange was balanced by the satisfaction he felt when
his highly practiced eye detected the delicate difference
on the back of the cards. The colorfully shaded feathers
of a peacock's spread tail had been subtly altered.

Rod calculated that the marking followed the simplest
possible pattern, matching his estimate of his opponents'
intelligence. From left to right, the first feather slightly
darkened would be an ace, the second a king, and so on.

Iron control and endless practice kept his lips from
assuming a sour expression of contempt. The fools. They
introduced a stacked deck without having carefully
warmed it in a pocket close to the body, and they com-
pounded their ineptness by having so crudely marked the
deck in the first place. As part of his long apprenticeship,

Rod had studied cards so expertly marked that it took him hours of concentrated effort to find the tampering. These he detected before the dealer finished distributing the cards. Rod's father would have had these men's arms broken and the men thrown naked into the nearest garbage heap.

Rod felt the familiar thrill, clear as a seductive siren's call, the instant his sensitive fingertips touched the first card of the hand being dealt. The time to strike had come, the moment Rod believed his special skills came into full focus.

Predators come into the world with physical and mental traits different from those inherited by their prey. A singularly important feature of the successful predator lies in a deep-seated instinct, brought to a fine edge by training and experience, to detect the precise moment to attack, to go for the jugular, to kill.

Heavyset and sweating in the trapped heat of the ship cabin—although it was still early in 1871, the sun had burned fiercely on the Gulf of Mexico that afternoon— the dealer followed the familiar game plan of the long-time, small-time card cheat. He tried to distract attention with small talk while spinning the cards across the table with flashy speed and accuracy. "Too bad you have to withdraw so early, sir. The game seldom gets really interesting until after midnight." His voice carried a poorly covered trace of scorn.

Rod, his cards pulled close and already hidden under his left hand, answered slowly, formally, as if he measured and weighed every word. "As I explained at the beginning, I live with the burden of delicate health. My father demands that I retire at midnight."

These men would never confess weakness and lack of independence so openly, and Rod expected them to feel a stir of disdain for a man who did. That impression was clouding their judgment, prompting them to think his winnings sprang from luck rather than skill. He enjoyed taking money from players who underestimated him. The lie, voiced in his habitual soft and deferential tone, caused a brief, embarrassed silence, and Rod savored the impact. The other six players studied their cards.

The small, pointy-faced man to Rod's left spoke in his irksome high voice, the squeak of a human ferret. "I'd be eager to leave too if I was winning as much as you." The man seemed unable to sit still; he presented a study in nervous fidgets and irritable complaints. Rod thought he worked too hard at his job and had identified him as the decoy at the table before the second hand had been dealt. The jittery mannerisms created as constant a distraction as a fire in a circus tent. This made the work of the fat card mechanic easier.

Broadman, the heavy-shouldered man across the table from Rod, spread his sun-darkened hands and, glancing at Ferret-Face, spoke gruffly. "Leave him alone, Mr. Leach. The man warned us before the first card hit the table. He said midnight was his bedtime." He shifted his gaze to look squarely at Rod. "You do look a little pale, Mr. Silvana, even for a man with yellow hair. You better buy you a good hat with a wide brim out here. The sun will burn you up in Texas."

Seven men were sitting in the game. Draw poker. No wild cards. No limit. Playing since six o'clock, Rod felt sure he had been fattened for the kill. Without touching his purposely sloppy pile of chips, he knew he stood slightly over five hundred dollars ahead. They needed to hook him now, before he left the game at midnight, and they had waited almost too long.

The fat dealer, Furnam, and the man to his right, Leach, were working together. Rod sat in the chair to the right of the two sharpers. He felt confident that the other men in the game played straight. The fat, jolly dealer with his skinny, jumpy partner had fallen into an old and much-overworked pattern. The two must have devised the plan to use the smaller man's abrasive complaints, usually directed toward his massive partner, to disguise their alliance and cover their efforts to control the cards.

Transparent. Pitiful. Not good enough to fool an alert
New Orleans schoolboy.

The deal completed, Rod examined his cards, palming
the hand to hide the backs from view. Four nines and a
stray ten. Broadman, to the left of the dealer, opened.
"I'll bet fifty." The three following players dropped out,
all of them nursing sadly diminished stacks of chips.

Rod, cards now on the table under his hand, said, "I'll
see your fifty and raise five hundred."

One player whistled and the others sat up straighter
and leaned forward. Leach's ferret face poorly concealed
the glint of greed in his eyes as he quickly—too
quickly—reached for his pocketbook. "That's five hundred and fifty to me, I believe. I'll see that and raise a
thousand."

He counted out the money and shoved it to the center
of the table, but with pretended awkwardness of nervous
hands handling both his cards and his wallet, he spread
his cards just enough to expose three tens to Rod. He
squeezed his cards together quickly and lowered them,
but he cast a sly glance at Rod to be sure the fake blunder
had been seen.

Furnam dropped his hand with a big show of relief and
said, "Too rich for me." Broadman threw in his cards
without comment.

Rod said, "Call." He counted out ten hundreds from
his pocketbook.

"Cards?"

Rod said, "Two."

"Two?" Furnam's eyes widened, and he actually
flinched. He could hardly have looked more astounded if
Rod had slapped him.

Rod glanced at Broadman and nodded slightly. Broadman rubbed the back of his neck and four men at an
adjoining table rose and approached.

"You want two?" Furnam's tone stopped barely short
of shouting: Look at your cards again, you fool!

Rod said quietly, "Yes, two please, dealt slowly."

Furnam's florid face stiffened. "What does that mean? Are you accusing me . . ."

Broadman deliberately drew a double-barreled derringer from his vest. "Deal, Mr. Furnam." He centered his hands in front of him on the table. His left hand, laid over his right, concealed the small weapon except for the pair of muzzles, now visible only from Rod's side of the table, aimed at the narrow empty space between Furnam and Leach. The other players froze, and the usual small talk ceased.

Furnam dealt Rod two cards.

Leach seemed to shrink, his eyes jerking like a cornered rodent. He licked his lips and slid his discards onto the table. "Two for me."

Rod could only see the back of the top card of Leach's two discards, but he read it marked as a ten. His relaxed posture no longer a pretense, he felt a surge of confidence that he had correctly guessed the path his prey would follow. The fool's mind had grown so locked on the original plan, and on the yawning barrels of the vicious little weapon facing him, that he threw away one of the key tens that would have won for him.

Had he been a worthy opponent, he would have held his three tens and taken his chances, knowing that Rod now held only three nines. Instead, shaken by the unexpected, he stuck to the original plan, even though it could no longer succeed, hoping the dealer could save him. The door to his trap closed so emphatically Rod wondered if the other players heard the echo. Now, with the prey in the trap, the only decision remaining lay in resolving how long to play with the victim.

Rod figured Furnam and Leach had stacked the deck confident that Rod would discard his useless ten. They certainly wouldn't expect him to stand pat on the hand. His obvious choice, to discard only the ten, would signal that the cards he held needed help, thus drawing other players into bidding against the implied four of a kind.

The sharpers never dreamed Rod would discard one of his four nines.

By exposing his three tens, Leach had intended to make Rod believe himself in control, "holding the hammer," with Leach's fourth ten captured in his own hand. Rod was supposed to bet wildly, confident that his four nines would defeat any draw possible for Leach. Leach planned to discard two of the decoy tens and draw two cards to fill a royal flush from the stacked deck. Rod's extra and totally unexpected discard disrupted the carefully stacked deck by pulling into his own hand one of the cards Leach had to have.

Without looking at his own cards, Rod fixed his eyes on the dealer and said, "Once again, sir, very, very slowly please." When Furnam had placed the cards in front of Leach, Rod added, "I'll bet another thousand."

Leach looked at his cards, a tic twitching at the corner of his eye. He sent a quick, desperate glance at Furnam before he said, "I don't have enough to cover. I guess you've bought yourself a pot."

Silence fell for about five seconds. Nobody moved.

Rod asked, "You withdraw, sir? I want to hear your decision plainly."

Leach threw his cards on the table and said, "I'm out. It's yours."

Broadman said, "You end the evening with a mystery hand, Mr. Silvana. I'd sure like to see your cards, but the cost got too steep for me."

"In this special case, I'll oblige you, sir. This hand will interest all of you."

Furnam reached forward to pull in the cards. "That hand's finished. Nobody—"

The double click when Broadman cocked the twin hammers of his derringer stopped Furnam in midsentence, his hands suspended over the table. One of the other players, perceiving the tiny weapon in Broadman's big hands for the first time, exclaimed, "My God, what . . . ?"

Another said, "Be quiet, man! For heaven's sake keep still."

Rod gently shoved Furnam's hands aside, retrieved his own discards, and threw them and his hand faceup on the table. Before Furnam or Leach could react, he did the same with Leach's cards.

"Gentlemen, had I not thrown one of my nines, this queen would have gone to Mr. Leach." He slipped the queen into place to complete the royal flush. "Mr. Leach panicked and followed a plan gone wrong. He threw away two of his three tens, after pretending an accident to be sure I saw them, to get his royal flush. If he'd had the presence of mind to hold his tens, knowing I had discarded one of my nines, he would have won. I think your little pistol upset him, Mr. Broadman."

The four men, at Broadman's signal, had positioned themselves around the table behind the players. Broadman said, "We've had complaints. I'm a professional gambler, gentlemen. Passengers have complained to the shipowners, so they hired me to investigate, but Mr. Silvana did my job for me."

Rod continued. "I noticed that someone cold-decked us, and I saw that the new cards were marked. Please note the conveniently darkened peacock feathers."

Broadman's attention never wavered from Leach and Furnam. When the other men picked up cards, examined them, and shook their heads, Rod gathered several face cards. "If you'll riffle the cards and watch the peacock feathers, you'll see that a dark feather seems to dance around." He sat patiently while the men performed the experiment. Each nodded after a couple of tries.

"Of course, since no player has left the table, I assume all of you gentlemen are willing to be searched to find the exchanged deck."

Leach said, "This is nonsense I'll not stand for such an insult." But when he rose, the man behind him pinned his arms. Another stepped forward and ran his hands expertly across Leach's clothing. He eased a deck of cards from the struggling little man's coat and placed them on the table. Another of the men pulled a sleeve gun and a pocket derringer from the seated Furnam and dropped them into his own coat pockets. Leach sank back into his chair.

Rod removed his own money from the chips and currency in the center of the table and shoved back the remainder. He glanced at the other players and said, "Gentlemen, we can only prove what happened on this particular hand, but we must assume the play has been crooked all evening. I guess each of you knows how much you put in the game. I'll ask you to be on your honor to retrieve only what you lost. Then I shall be most pleased to accept the rest of the money contributed by these two cheats."

The division completed, Rod asked, "Everybody satisfied?" Without waiting for an answer, he spun a ten-dollar gold piece to the center of the table. "Have a drink on me, gentlemen."

Broadman said, "Join us. One drink won't hurt you."

"My sincere regrets, sir. But as I said before, my health won't allow hard spirits, none at all."

Furnam, his bloated face pale with fury, struggled to rise against the restraining hands of one of Broadman's four men. "You sissified little snake. It's a good thing you've got a gang to help you. I'd blow your head off."

"I assume you handle guns better than cards, Mr. Furnam. You should stick to what you do best. Make your living as an assassin." Rod backed away from the table, moved to the door with his eyes still on Furnam, and left the room.

Broadman snapped curt instructions to his men and followed, finding Rod just outside the door waiting for his eyes to adjust to the darkness. In the pitch-black of the deck, his voice barely carried over the slap of water on the hull. "We'll be in Indianola tomorrow, Mr. Silvana. I think you should book passage back to New Orleans or somewhere as soon as you can."

Rod turned to face the big man when he continued to speak.

"Indianola's a rough town in a violent state. Take Furnam's threat seriously. Men commonly carry guns in Texas. Texans regard theft of a horse a more serious offense than killing a man, unless he's unarmed. The Army's still in control of the whole state, so Texans despise the law. They fight everybody in reach—Mexicans, Comanches, Apaches, and if nobody else is handy, they fight each other."

"Mr. Broadman, my father is a gambler, among many other things. He trained me in the craft since I was a child of six. He also saw to it that I had jobs as a youth to instill in me a distaste for hard physical labor. Once, he sent me to work in a slaughterhouse for several months during a hot summer. I learned to despise killing helpless creatures, but I also understand that it's necessary, and one must become hardened to it. I would have regretted killing Furnam and Leach this evening, but if required, I would have done so."

"That would have surprised me an hour ago, but it doesn't now. When you nodded to me during the game, I don't know how, but I understood your signal at once. I felt no concern that you might embarrass me by being wrong. How did you know what I was there for?"

"Your men weren't clever enough. All of them were trying to watch you. If you'd have them sit farther apart in the future, an observer won't have such an easy time noticing. Only one of them needs to keep his eyes on you. The others can watch him. At a signal, they can switch the duty of watching you, so nobody seems to stare impolitely."

When Rod opened the door to his stateroom and lighted the hanging coal oil lamp, the flare of the match caught Broadman's sour expression before he could conceal it. "Don't worry about those two crooks. We'll take care of them for the rest of the cruise, but I think that fellow Furnam is stupid enough to be dangerous. He might pursue the matter onshore."

"Thank you, Mr. Broadman, but I never worry. I believe in planning but not worrying."

"You don't care what happens to those two? You're not even curious, are you?"

"No, I believe I already have most of their money. Good night, sir."

Broadman nodded and turned away. Rod closed the door.

TWO

RODRIGO VASQUEZ ALLESANDRO Castillo y Silvana sat in his luxurious study, his unseeing gaze fixed
on the polished top of his desk. Slowly his eyes closed as
his head dropped forward to meet the fingers of his left
hand.

Never could a man have a more respectful and
obedient son than Rodrigo had in Rod, and never could
a father have planned his son's training and guidance
more carefully. He had spent money without restraint,
had hired the best tutors and coaches. Yet, something had
gone terribly wrong.

His eldest son, physically the image of his father, had
become a coldly efficient instrument. A deadly accurate
marksman with rifle and pistol, graceful and tall in the
saddle, fluent in three languages, adept with accounting,
and with an already mature head for business, he seemed
to those outside the family to be the perfect first-born
son, the classic scion in the aristocratic tradition.

Yet, the words "coldly efficient" rang in Rodrigo's

mind over and over. The boy, warmly affectionate in the family, showed no heart outside, deliberately made no intimate friends. Although he seemed to gain respect easily and always received more social invitations than he could honor, he ignored those who tried to get close to him. And Rodrigo knew the blame fell on his own shoulders. His beloved son followed his father's advice, but he did so too well, too thoroughly.

Rodrigo, without opening his eyes, sat back in the chair and rolled his head in a circle several times, first to the left and then back again to the right. His tense neck popped like a nervous idiot cracking his knuckles. Involuntarily both hands rose to massage the tight muscles behind his ears.

Unwittingly, he had created a cynic, a cold loner. His repeated warnings to his son had been heeded too well. How often had he warned: Never lend money to a friend unless you want him for an enemy. . . . Never give anything away in business or at the gaming tables. . . . Never let anyone know your thoughts unless you're willing to have them used against you. . . . Most men are not intentionally treacherous, just easily tempted, so be on your guard.

Rodrigo remembered the care with which he'd placed a deck of cards in his son's hands on the boy's sixth birthday. The key to success often lay in simple alertness, and he knew no better way to develop the skill to analyze one's competitors than at a poker table. He'd said, "Son, poker is a civilized method of dueling. Only winners can prosper, only winners."

Regularly, he had hired or forced gamblers to come to the Silvana home and spend long hours sharing their secrets with Rod, skills akin to magic gained by endless hours of practice. Rodrigo regarded skill at cards as an emergency last resort for a gentleman, a way to make money without working with his hands. Physical work was the ultimate degradation for an aristocrat.

Rod succeeded through a rigid, self-imposed disci-

pline still a source of surprise to Rodrigo. While still a
child, Rod had allotted an hour of each day to practice
and had imperiously ordered the servants to buy three
large mirrors so he could watch his own hands when he
manipulated the cards.

Upon his return from his most recent four-year tour in
Spain, England, and France, he casually returned the
funds Rodrigo had provided for the trip. Rod had indeed
followed instructions. He'd introduced himself to the
Silvana relatives in Spain, had ingratiated himself with a
long list of aristocratic and commercial contacts in
England and France, and had evidently enjoyed a young
man's version of a wonderful vacation. With the smiling
confidence of the self-assured wealthy, he had sampled
the best of everything.

The funds came from sharp play at gaming tables in
London, Paris, Madrid, and many stops along the way.
Rodrigo's eldest son had become a gambler, as grimly
efficient as a scalpel, with a tireless alertness supported
by an iron-hard body. Rod imposed on himself an
inflexible schedule in the finest gymnasiums and sport-
ing clubs, devoting part of virtually every day to vigor-
ous exercise.

But Rod had never done a day's work in his life,
except for an unpleasant assignment one summer in a
slaughterhouse. Rodrigo had reasoned that a few months
of unpleasant labor would inspire his son to appreciate
his station in life and add a maturing influence. The only
observable impact on Rod from that experience had been
a curiously heightened respect for the damage a trained
man could do with a small knife. Since then, Rod had
never been without a wicked little blade hidden somewhere on his person.

Rodrigo felt he must craft a new challenge for his son,
one that would awaken Rod to the requirements of this
fast-changing American society. The old world ways of
the aristocracy drew contempt on this side of the Atlantic, a fact Rodrigo recognized that he, himself, had been

too slow to acknowledge. Rod needed to learn to understand and appreciate commoners if he were to succeed in this country, and these common men differed sharply from those in Europe.

Rodrigo shuddered, the involuntary flinch vibrating through his long frame. The father had to devise a way to teach his son something the father had been painfully slow to learn himself. He well knew Rod looked upon him as an idol, the perfectly successful man. Yet, Rodrigo knew his own ways were of the past. Comfortable in Europe, he found himself often ill at ease among Americans, even in New Orleans, which clung to its old-world flavor.

He needed to add something to his son's character that he knew had been too slow to develop in his own. Rodrigo had never understood simple kindness outside his own family. As he grew older, he saw that defect with clear-eyed regret, and he feared he had created a son in his own image who carried the same flaw.

He picked up the letter lying on his desk and read it again, for perhaps the tenth time. The letter carried the signature of Milton Baynes, a nephew, son of his sister and the rough but sturdy and crafty American she'd eloped with and loved until the day she died. His sister had learned fast, or she'd had more finely tuned instincts. She had spurned the aristocratic tradition and married against all attempts to dissuade her. Her sons were perfectly adapted to succeed in this raw, new land, and succeed they had. And her commoner husband, Darnell Baynes, a man with calluses on his hands, had become the best friend Rodrigo ever had.

Milton's letter suggested that cattle offered the best investment in the country, the first compelling commercial bonding between the defeated Confederacy and the victorious Union. Gathered in Texas, the half-wild beasts could be bought for eight dollars or less, driven to Kansas, and sold there for as much as thirty dollars, sometimes even a bit more. In money-starved Texas, drovers could be hired for almost nothing.

Milton, with the brash confidence of resourceful men in this new world, described a highly speculative investment, with many potential hazards, as if it were routine. He spoke of several grinding months on the trail with the cheerful disregard of a hardened frontiersman.

Rodrigo's stomach tightened at the thought of his soft-handed, immaculately dressed son spending long days in the saddle, burned by sun and chilled by rain, all the while in the company of illiterate, coarse riffraff. Impulsively he opened the lower drawer of his desk and reached for a small packet of letters.

His hand stopped short, and he slowly slid the drawer shut again. More than a dozen letters from associates and family in Europe lay in that drawer, expressing concern about Rod, about altercations in "low dens of iniquity" where men were injured and killed. He had never managed to question Rod about those letters, but he knew his son's contact with the lower classes had not been without incident. Yes, the change in Rod since his return had not been missed by his fatherly eye. Something about the young man discouraged questions.

Rod no longer entered a room without quickly but thoroughly identifying everyone present. He deftly adjusted his stance to put a wall to his back. His cold alertness, evidently not observed by others, came easily to Rodrigo's notice.

Lukie had changed even more. He no longer seemed the nonchalant, lifetime servant. Above his smile, a quiet calculation lay behind his eyes, an icy alertness. Rodrigo searched for a term to describe the new Lukie. Confederate, perhaps? Bodyguard?

Could this challenge in Texas be the final item on a list of experiences his son needed to become a true man in this new country? Could he lead such independent, disrespectful rabble, many of them battle-hardened veterans who now carried weapons as a matter of habit? Was it worth the risk? Milton made it plain that a cattle drive presented serious dangers, many potentially fatal.

A light tap on the door sent a shock of added tension through Rodrigo. He took a deep, slow breath. The time for decision had come.

"Come in."

Rod entered and stood respectfully until his father gestured for him to take a seat in front of the desk. The tall black man who followed him into the room closed the door and stood still as a statue in front of it.

"Son, on the advice of your Cousin Milton, I've decided to undertake a speculative venture. I propose to buy cattle in Texas and drive them to market in Kansas."

Rod sat at ease in the straight chair, perfectly manicured fingers laced together in his lap. His expression showed only courteous attention.

"Milton says a herd of three thousand is practical. He's made the trip successfully twice. He'll be driving his own, but he says he can hire competent men to gather and drive our herd. I've already sent funds to him to start gathering our cattle. The money involved is considerable. At eight dollars each, a herd of three thousand will cost twenty-four thousand dollars. Milton says the costs involved in paying drovers and for food and other expenses should run about two to four dollars per animal. A thirty-thousand-dollar investment may return as much as ninety thousand in Kansas if prices hold up. There's a good chance I can triple our money in a matter of months."

Rod nodded. "It sounds good." His tone betrayed only polite interest.

"Milton's generous offer takes too much on his shoulders, son. He has his own herd to tend. I want you to go to Texas and supervise our investment."

Rod's expression remained unchanged. Rodrigo came to a new level of appreciation for his son's masterful facial control. The gambler never blinked, and his answer came without hesitation.

"I can do that, sir, but I know nothing about cattle, nothing at all."

Rodrigo sat quietly for a moment, staring at the son so much like him. His next words, spoken gently, carried the iron sound of an armored gauntlet thrown on his desk. "Of course, I understand. If you don't feel qualified, I couldn't ask you to take the responsibility."

When Rod's eyes briefly met his, Rodrigo felt a surge of satisfaction. The directness of the glance resembled the fixed attention of a man aligning sights, but his son's easy smile warmed his heart. Rodrigo savored the soaring joy of pride in his firstborn, a calculating man in perfect control of himself, who read and understood his father's intentions without the need for undignified and demeaning conversation.

Rod came to his feet and gestured toward Milt's letter. When Rodrigo handed it to him, he asked, "Is that all for now, sir?" At Rodrigo's nod, he added, "I'll study Cousin Milton's letter and return it to you, sir." At the door, he turned. "I'll arrange passage for Texas at once."

The door closed behind him, but the tall black man still stood in the shadows. "Do your best, Lukie." A brief nod, and the man stepped out.

After the door clicked shut again, Rodrigo stared at it for a moment. The failure of three banks and the loss of ships trying to run the Yankee blockade during the war had severely damaged the Silvana fortune. Unless this venture prospered, he would have to seek credit, put strategic assets in jeopardy, and risk shaking the confidence of essential backers. Although they had never discussed the present financial crisis, Rodrigo respected his son's ability to read numbers, and he knew his son took an interest in the ledgers of the family's investments. Rod knew his success or failure might determine the course of the Silvanas' financial future.

Rodrigo whispered, "Good luck, my son."

• • •

Rod fought down a feeling of distaste. Indianola, touted to have the climate of paradise, looked like nothing more than a long, trashy sandbar waiting for the next high wave to wash it clean. Considered to have the finest harbor on the Gulf of Mexico, the busy port city didn't look like much, even though much of it had been rebuilt after heavy damage from a terrible storm in 1866. No grace, no style here. The town resembled plain white boxes dropped from a careless hand onto a flat, boring plain.

He shrugged under his expensive English linen coat, tailored to a loose fit to mask his muscular frame and to conceal twin derringers. Business must be done where profit beckoned, even along a mosquito-infested coastline threatened by yellow fever and deadly storms.

As the craft neared one of the piers stretching half a mile into the bay, the other passengers turned away from their first view of the most important port in Texas. Surprised exclamations seemed to roll along the rail like a wave while Broadman's men dragged the struggling and protesting Leach and Furnam to the rail. Both wore coal-blackened clothing and swollen, bruised faces. Broadman walked over to stand beside Rod, both feet planted solidly on the deck, hands behind his back.

Furnam rolled a vicious eye toward Rod and shouted, "I'll find you, and I'll kill you for this, you prissy bastard."

Rod turned and looked at Broadman. The other passengers did the same, fooled into thinking him the target of the insult.

"Clever, Mr. Silvana, very clever. You know how to avoid attention, don't you?" Broadman bowed his head mockingly toward the two disheveled gamblers. "My men knocked them around a little bit, just to emphasize our displeasure with them. Then our two cheats spent a memorable night bound and gagged on the floor of the boiler room. Made them both cranky."

Broadman made a small gesture with his thumb. At the signal, his men threw the cursing pair over the side. As soon as the flailing bodies struck the water, Broadman's men raced toward the stern and tried to hit the pair of bobbing heads with their own luggage.

"Can they swim?"

Broadman stepped to the rail and leaned out to look. "Never thought to ask. Does it matter?"

"No, just curious."

"We waited to get close enough to shore for them to make it to dry land or a pier. The captain asked us to tarry until broad daylight so the passengers could see them hit the water. I guess he figured that would help get word around that this ship is no place for card cheats."

Rod nodded. "Better than printing it in a newspaper. A good story told in the bars gets to those folks who don't read much."

"You better watch for that fat one, Mr. Silvana. He thinks himself to be tough. He's the kind to carry a grudge like a badge of honor. I fear he'll look for you."

"As you said yourself when he hit the water, does it matter?"

Broadman studied Rod thoughtfully for a moment before he answered. "You had us all fooled. You're a cold one, aren't you?"

"I hope not, sir, just practical."

"Will you be in Indianola long, Mr. Silvana?"

"Probably not. I'm looking into a business opportunity on behalf of my father."

"Alone? I mean, you look a bit young and . . ."

"Defenseless?"

"Well, yeah, to tell the truth."

"Have you ever been to the part of London known as the East End, Mr. Broadman?"

"No, but I've heard of it."

"As part of my education, I spent several months there, making my own way. I'm twenty-four years old, Mr. Broadman, and my father has unusual ideas about the training his sons should have. He thinks every man should be prepared to face what can be a hard life."

"You made your way with cards?"

"How else? Many aristocratic and wealthy English gentlemen from the West End go there to gamble, to drink, and, of course, to sample the whores. They had money to spare, and I needed it."

"Well, I wish you luck, sir." Broadman suddenly broke into laughter. "It seems my concern about you was misplaced."

"May we meet again soon." Rod offered his hand and Broadman took it with a firm grasp and a searching expression.

After Broadman joined his men at the stern, Rod stood alone, eyes narrowed against the brilliant Texas sun, watching the pier draw nearer. That searching expression in the eyes of newly met people had become routine. Rod knew that his blond hair, blue eyes, and smooth complexion made him look younger than his years and seemed to belie his Spanish ancestry. He often made himself shake hands timidly, seeking to avoid the curiosity aroused when men felt the contrast of a heavy-boned, powerful grip from a hard hand without calluses.

Rod wore a mask. He had convinced himself while still a child that, in any competition, surprise usually made an enormous difference. To be underestimated provided an often decisive advantage. Thus, his broad shoulders and muscular frame stayed hidden under clothing tailored to conceal. Tailors threw up their hands in dismay at his demand to appear like an expensively dressed lump.

At the landing, he pulled on kidskin gloves and waited patiently while porters loaded his trunks onto a coach. As usual, he ignored curious glances from passengers. Rod's patient, empty-handed stance signaled the world that he had no intention of lifting or carrying anything, and his stack of sturdy trunks differed sharply from the meager packages of most of the other passengers.

At the raised brow of the coachman, he said simply, "The best lodgings in town, sir."

Seated beside the driver, Rod nodded to the tall black man standing nearby. The man nimbly climbed aboard and settled himself on one of Rod's trunks. Years had passed since Lukie had handled baggage, except in perfect privacy.

THREE

MILTON BAYNES RODE with the casual grace of the born horseman, habit steering his actions while his thoughts ranged elsewhere. He eased Judas, now an aging favorite, along the rutted dirt trail toward Victoria. Judas, equally a creature of habit, tried half-heartedly to reach his rider's knee with yellowed teeth and got a jerk on the reins and a swat on an ear from his rider's hat for his trouble.

"Quit that, you sorry old devil."

Judas slicked the punished ear. The formalities satisfied, the ride could proceed routinely for an hour or so unless he found a rare unguarded opportunity to show his meanness.

One of Milt's Texas-bred Mexican riders had brought the word yesterday that Rod Silvana had arrived in Victoria and would be coming to the ranch today. Hospitality demanded that he be met and welcomed at about the halfway point of the day-long ride. The custom gave Milt a perfect opportunity to talk to Rod without

Cris hearing. Milt idly rubbed the back of his neck, tipping his wide-brimmed hat forward.

He still felt surprise and a touch of amusement every time his hand found no braid of hair extending down his back. His neat haircut reminded him more strongly than his wedding ring of Cris, his strong-minded, fiery-haired wife. She liked his hair shorter, so he wore it like she preferred. In fact, she insisted on cutting it herself. Every time he touched the back of his neck, he thought of her and grinned. She caught him doing it several times, read his mind, and grinned right back.

Milt's chance to chat with Rod for almost half a day on the ride back home would fill him with information Cris wouldn't know. She hated having to ask him anything but couldn't help being as curious as a chipmunk. This opportunity represented perfection under a blue sky. He'd have a chance to use every evasive retort he could conjure up, drive her to distraction with vague answers, and give them both hours of entertainment before she gouged every detail out of him.

Milt felt mildly shocked when he realized he hadn't seen Rod since 1862, nine years ago. He did some figuring on the fingertips of his free hand to verify that Rod must have been fifteen then. Milt idly shook his head at the wonders in his family. Darnell Baynes hated gambling, and Rodrigo Silvana, among other business interests, ran two gambling houses in New Orleans. Darnell strongly discouraged his boys from even touching a deck of cards, wouldn't tolerate having them in the house. Rodrigo insisted that young Rod be trained in card handling, hired the best men available to tutor him in the skill, and encouraged him to practice regularly. Yet, Darnell and Rodrigo, in spite of having conflicting views on so many things, enjoyed a special bond far beyond their relationship as brothers-in-law.

Still, on major issues, Milt saw common ground in some of the decisions made by his uncle and his father. Both man went to extreme lengths to keep their sons out of the Civil War. Darnell abandoned his home and took his sons west. Rodrigo sent young Rod to Mexico, Spain, England, and heaven knew where else. Milt often wondered how Rod had managed to avoid demands that he return home and serve in the military. Maybe nobody paid attention to a rich young man traveling overseas from a country wracked by civil war, but that seemed unlikely. Perhaps, because Rod still looked so much younger than his years, the question never arose. The answer probably met the demands of simplicity. Rod, simply, knew how to do it.

Rod knew how to do all kinds of tricks. Milt grinned as he wondered if he could still palm and switch dice the way Rod taught him during one of the frequent Baynes family visits to New Orleans. How long ago had that happened? Twelve years? Fourteen?

Milt guided Judas off the road into a clump of trees when he neared the crest of a long, low rise. It made a man more comfortable to know what lay on the other side of a hill before he rode into it. Judas eased up to the crest and stopped behind a screen of brush.

Milt saw a wagon approaching, still a mile or so away. He pulled his binoculars from their square leather case and took a long look. Two saddled horses followed the rig. Two men rode the wide seat, but another man walked beside the wagon, if that could be called walking. Arms and legs pumping, the figure looked like a frantic puppet with its strings pulled by an excited child.

Puzzled, Milt scanned the area thoroughly before he tucked the binoculars away. If his horse had gone lame, the walker could still have taken a ride on the wagon. Nobody in Texas walked if he could help it, not even children. Little mysteries made Milt uncomfortable and skittish.

He eased Judas farther into the grove and found a vantage point where he could observe the approaching wagon when it came around the last bend before the crest. Mysteries like this often led to surprises, and surprises mostly led to trouble of one sort or another. Nothing wrong with taking a closer look before riding into sight.

The winding road took the rig from view among the trees, and Milt used the time to check the loads in his Navy, holster it, and unboot his Spencer for a quick examination. He unshucked his binoculars again. Before raising them, he slowly and carefully scanned the ground closest to him. When he raised the binoculars, he scanned the close terrain again before methodically examining the more distant ground in overlapping sweeps, gradually moving each sweep to a greater range. Even the dumbest of the dumb knows that a close threat offers more danger than a distant one. Milt scanned the closest land yet again. Nothing suspicious.

The hill sank into ominous quiet. An old campaigner, Judas stood absolutely motionless, matching the stillness of his rider. Milt's firm hand on his neck furnished a clear signal his rider would tolerate none of his foolishness. He earned his oats and forgiveness for his irascible nature by displaying iron discipline when he felt this kind of tension from the man he carried. Milt claimed that Judas was the steadiest gun horse in the world, and perfect stability under the saddle now proved the point.

Milt itched with suspicion. The wagon should have rolled into sight by now. Like all watchers, Milt hated to be seen unless he chose to be, and like all ambushers, he smelled traps everywhere. Milt suspected the walker or the men on the wagon might have caught a glimpse of him and they might have circled to catch him from an unexpected direction. He dropped the reins to the ground, knowing Judas would stand steady, and slid gently to the soft earth. He could do his own circling, and he liked to be moving anyway.

The draw offered the only chance for a trap. It was the only route leading to Milt's lookout point by which a skillful sneak might try to approach unseen. That was the approach a trickster would have to take, so that had to be the place Milt could turn the tables. He crept toward a huge old oak, at least five feet thick at its base, which stood at the edge of a steep drop into the narrow draw. The draw led from lower ground almost to the top of the ridge and had a sandy bottom. Milt felt a tug of impatience at his slow progress. He had to move dry leaves one by one silently, and he knew the sandy bottom in the draw gave a careful man fast and silent footing.

Milt's heart nearly stopped. A curve in the draw just a few yards downstream allowed him to see the sandy bottom. Tracks showed as plain as a row of biscuits on a table. A tiny scratch, just a hint of noise, like a squirrel on the other side of the tree, froze Milt in place, afraid to draw a decent breath. He'd guessed right. His man had come up the draw and now stood on the other side of the oak.

Milt knew he rode a lucky streak. He'd arrived before his man had a chance to glance over the top. A second or two later and he'd have been caught in the open, picking up and putting down leaves like a dunce.

Time to gamble. Milt bet himself the man would take a peep and then climb out of the draw around the left side of the tree, the sure path if Milt faced a right-handed sneak. If he timed it perfectly, he could slip around the right side and catch his man flatfooted with his gun facing the wrong way. If he guessed wrong, he'd come face to face with the fellow. Navy in hand, Milt moved, legs and arms spread wide so no brushed cloth would give warning.

Two careful steps took him around the trunk to the brink of the draw, and he looked down and to his left. The man had started to climb out, but he had only swung one arm to the high ground. Milt could see his whole body except his head and one shoulder. Milt watched as one leg slowly straightened and the other foot, clad in an expensive, handmade English walking boot, gently searched for purchase on the slick slope among the exposed roots of the old tree.

With agonizing slowness, Milt pulled in a huge breath silently through his mouth and screamed, "Bang! Bang! I gotcha!"

With a startled howl, the rattled man's whole body flinched with the shock, a boot slipped on the damp, slick green slope, and he slid on his stomach to the sandy bed of the draw.

"Damn you, Milt. I think I pissed in my pants."

"You city boys are near-about helpless, Cousin Rod. You've lost all your animal instincts. I had two clean, point-blank shots right at your little pink butt. You'd never sit straight again if I wasn't a man of mercy."

Rod brushed at green streaks on his trousers. "Look what you made me do. Grass stains never come out. You know what these pants cost?"

"I'll never forgive myself." Milt holstered his Navy, jumped into the little draw, and threw his arms around his kinsman. The world spun out of control, and he landed flat on his back with Rod on top of him.

"One, two, three. That's one fall. Want to go for two out of three?" Rod sprang up and lifted Milt to his feet.

"No fair. Your butt's full of lead. You got no right to be throwing me while I'm trying to be a genial host. You should be sticking fingers in the holes in your ass to keep from leaking to death."

Rod's hand held Milt's in an iron grip. "You look great, Milt. I've missed you more than you'll ever know. My heart's so happy I might haul off and cry."

Milt threw his free arm around Rod. "Me too. It's been too long." He turned Rod and nudged him up the slope toward where Judas stood hidden in the trees.

"I figured I'd surprise you. How'd you know?" Rod sounded irritated.

"You stopped the wagon. I smelled a trick."

Rod snapped his fingers. "I feared that, but the kid driving the wagon got all sweaty and shifty. He'd have warned you somehow if I let him get close enough. He kept saying you'd kill me, and he'd have to take the blame. Said the red demon would get him. He started sweating even more when I asked who the red demon was. Swore he never said that. Claimed I misunderstood him and apologized for his poor English. Who's he talking about?"

"My adoring wife. You'll meet her soon's we get to the house. Prettiest thing you ever saw in female form, but she's a demon rightly enough."

"I thought that young man said he worked on your place. He said he'd been sent to Victoria to get me."

"Yeah, he's one of our people."

"You let servants speak of your wife that way?"

"Servants?" Milt shook his head. "No, it doesn't work that way in Texas. It's not like New Orleans. These people aren't like servants at all. They're more like a big family. They work on the ranch and draw wages, but they own part of it too. Caleb Cowan, the old man we bought the place from, kept part of the land and deeded it to his hands. They own their own homes. Cowan is an uncle to Cris. The old man stays on because Cris and her brother are the only kinfolk he has. He's teaching me what I need to know about the cattle business. I guess I'm not explaining this very well. Just take my word for it. We have a special situation out here, but it works out mighty nice. I started all this red demon stuff by teasing Cris. The hands picked it up from me. It's kind of a joke we share. No harm intended. By the way, how'd you figure I'd be on that hill waiting for you?"

"Your man told me you'd probably meet us about halfway to the ranch. I figured you never grew up, so you'd be laying an ambush."

"Nothing like being predictable."

"Milt, you've always been predictably unpredictable. But I figured you'd come up with some way to raise hell with me. You always do that, you know, with everybody."

"You ready to become a cowman?"

"I look forward to it about like meeting a hangman. Sounds like work."

"What were you doing staggering around by the wagon? I saw you with my binoculars. Looked like you were having a seizure."

"Race walking. Learned it in England. Great fun once you get the hang of it. Every young Englishman who claims to be physically fit has to be able to walk forty miles in a day."

"Sure. And they can jump a hundred feet straight up and swim a hundred miles against a strong current."

"No fooling, Milt. I can do it. It's not as hard as it sounds if you keep fit. Rumor has it that Lord Byron could do it, even though he hated walking and was known to be terribly sensitive because he had a bad leg or a clubfoot or something of that sort. I heard that Stonewall Jackson could move his infantry forty miles a day. Didn't they call them his walking cavalry?"

"Who's Stonewall Jackson?"

Rod shook his head. "Ah, me. I was afraid you'd grown up and gained a little dignity, but I see now I shouldn't have worried."

"I may be a buffoon, but I'm too smart to walk when my cousin sends me a good saddle horse. Now we'll have to watch that animal. After you insulted him like that, he'll kick you over the corral fence if we aren't careful."

"Riding is a pleasure, Milt, but after a few hours I get tired of it. I'd just as soon walk. Walking is better exercise anyway. I like to keep fit."

"That's good, Cousin. By the time we get to Kansas, you'll be so fit you won't know yourself. Soon's we get to the house, I'll have Cris start you to drinking goat milk."

"Goat milk? What're you talking about, Milt?"

"You got a lot of riding to do. Drinking goat milk will help you. You're going to need a hard butt."

Rod grimaced. "That was the worst joke I ever heard in my whole life."

When the two men approached, Judas saw his chance. He reached for Rod's arm. His teeth clicked together an inch short when Rod sprang back. "Milt, that beast tried to bite me!"

"I told you. He saw you walking too, with a good horse right there handy. Word'll get around. You won't find a friendly horse on the place an hour after we get home. When word gets around, they'll all want a bite of you."

Milt pulled his Navy, fired a shot in the air, and started reloading. "Rod, you just lay yourself down in the shade of that tree yonder and hold real still. Lay yourself down awkward and funny so you look good and dead. Let's scare the beans out of that kid I sent after you."

"I'll do it, but you hide, Milt. Don't show yourself before it's plain I'm just pretending. Lukie would kill you before you could blink."

"Oops. I forgot Lukie. Don't worry. I'll stay hid until you come back to life."

FOUR

"MEN ON A trail drive act just like a pirate crew." Caleb Cowan spoke to Rod like a man instructing a child. "They sign on to do what the boss says. They ride where he wants 'em to ride—point, flank, or drag. They don't vote on nothin'. You fire a man or he decides to quit, you don't make him walk the plank, but he walks off with no wages. You hear me, boy? He walks. He don't ride. The trail boss can't spare no horses. If a pirate ain't there when the booty gets divided, he don't exist. A rider quits before the herd is delivered and paid for, he don't exist neither. He don't get nothin'."

Rod, safe behind his gambler's mask, held himself in check. Cris's uncle seemed determined to show in every possible way that he found Rod to be useless, or worse, a liability. Rod nodded and said, "Noted. What if a man breaks his leg?"

The old man dropped his gaze for a second. "Well now, cases like that call for the trail boss to make a decision. If a man hurts himself on the job and ain't done nothin' stupid or silly to bring it on himself, the boss might drop him off at a homestead or a town to get himself well. The boss might give him enough money to get home. If he hurt himself acting dumb, doing some kind of horseplay or devilment, the boss might leave him sitting in the dust where he fell. It's up to the boss."

"Have you ever left a man like that?"

"Boy, men who work for me know where they stand. I ain't never had to leave nobody except one I shot."

"What happened?"

"He decided to quit, and he talked a couple of other riders into going with him. He told me they were going home, that they planned to take three horses, and he dared me to try to stop 'em. Damn fool—excuse me, Cris—figured himself to be a gunfighter or something. I shot him. To tell the story plain and straight, I shot him four times."

Milt, immobile as a statue, said, "Fired five times. Missed him once. Missed him clean."

Cowan directed a poisonous glance at Milt and asked, "You tellin' this or me?"

When Milt didn't answer immediately, Cris thumped him on the shoulder with her little fist and said, "Hush. Let Uncle Caleb tell his windy."

Cowan waited through about five seconds of silence before his gaze swung back to Rod. "I was walkin' toward him while I was shooting. Stepped in a hole and missed one shot. Milt, now, he's perfect. He never misses. That's the way it is when a person is perfect, you know. Ain't that right, Milt?"

Milt didn't answer but sat frozen, apparently fascinated by the fist Cris held in readiness above the table.

"Anyway, the other two men reconsidered while I had 'em digging a hole for that feller. They decided to finish the drive. Turned out to be handy men, too, once they knew my word was good. You don't have to be perfect"— Cowan's venomous glance probed Milt again—"but men got to trust your word in this country, or you can't do nothin' with 'em. They just ignore you."

"Seems to me free men have the right to quit any time they choose." Rod sipped the last of his coffee and gently replaced the dainty china cup on its saucer.

Cowan sneered. "That kind of thinking causes more trouble than rustlers. Nobody's free, son. Every man worth a pinch of salt has responsibilities. The only free man is one with no duties, has nobody depending on him, no friends who trust him. The man who has rights is the man who does the work. If he does the work, he has a right to his wages. A man says to me, 'I'll ride to Kansas with you,' then we get about up to the Indian Nations and he quits—his word ain't no good. When talk gets around and folks hear he done that, won't nobody in Texas hire him to clean an outhouse."

"What if a man gets killed? Run over by a steer or shot by an Indian?"

"We bury him decent as we can. We bring his wages home to his family, and we help his kin if they have need, say until his kids get old enough to work or his woman finds herself another man. A man can't ever be free, son, unless he walks away from responsibility, and those who do that ain't nothin' but piss in the wind—excuse me, Cris."

Rod nodded and silence fell. Milt and Cris sat at the table in the cool, dark living room, empty coffee cups in front of them. Cris always seemed to be active, her gray eyes moving back and forth between Caleb and Rod when they spoke, hands straightening her spoon, smoothing her dress, stroking the sleeping baby in her lap. She seemed to radiate boundless energy, restive but not nervous. Milt, in consummate contrast, remained motionless. Rod couldn't tell if Milt stayed awake or even continued to breathe.

Cowan asked, "You ever rope a steer?"

"No, sir."

"You ever brand a cow?"

"No, sir."

"What you plan to do on this drive? Cook?"

Rod smiled, although it took all his strength to do it. "I'm here at my father's request. He has a large investment in this enterprise. He thought I could help Milt."

Cowan's glare would have soured milk. "Large investment in this enterprise, eh?" He glanced at Milt. "Won't take much of that kind of talk to scatter a herd. They never heard such like."

Milt's comment came sudden and flat. "Rod can learn, Caleb."

Cowan's gaze swung back to Rod. "Soft hands, skin like milk."

Rod said, "Yes, sir. And a word, once given, that's good as gold in the pocket."

Cowan studied Rod, eye to eye, for several seconds before he relaxed and nodded. "I guess that'll have to be good enough for now, boy. We'll see how you fare soaking wet in the night wind, your pale hide scalded by a south Texas sun, covered with an inch of cow shit— excuse me, Cris—and after two or three days in the saddle without sleep."

Cris, straight-faced, spoke at last. "Cow shit—excuse me, Uncle Caleb—won't bother you much, Rod. I scrape it off myself and put it on my roses. They love it. Other times, I use dried chunks of it to burn Milt's breakfast bacon when we're out on the prairie and can't find wood."

Rod gave her a smile, sensing he had an ally. "I believe the main reason I'm here is that my father thinks Milt, like the rest of the Baynes clan, is mildly insane."

"No," she said, "he's the only one. The others have good sense."

Milt broke his trance by lifting his brows in a nearly invisible gesture, but he said nothing. Rod wouldn't have known for certain Milt had moved at all except for the appearance of a tiny wrinkle across his forehead.

"My father probably thinks Milt would feel responsible because he suggested this cattle drive idea. If something were to go wrong, he things Milt'd try to make up any loss out of his own pocket. Most business-men would find that notion a little crazy, but I think it worried my father. He sent me to take that load off Milt so he can look after his own affairs."

Cowan snapped, "Probably? Your father probably thinks? Don't you know, boy?"

"Mr. Cowan, my father asked me to come to Texas and go on this cattle drive to look after his interests. When my father makes a request, it isn't my custom to ask why. I just do it. I shall go on this drive and, if I stay alive and competent to sit in a saddle, I shall finish this drive. If you question that, sir, you waste your time and mine."

"Got your dander up, didn't I, boy?"

"Do I appear angry, sir?"

Cowan grinned. He seemed genuinely amused. This was his first display of anything but a stern expression since Rod rode in yesterday evening. "No. You just look blank, but you spoke up right sharp. You spend a lot of time looking blank, don't you, boy? I hear you think you're a gambler, so you don't want to show nothin'."

"No, sir, I don't think I'm a gambler. I know. Would you like a demonstration?"

"Sure, boy. We ain't doin' nothin' but waitin' for supper."

"Fine." Rod pulled a deck from his coat pocket and had his thumb poised to break the seal when Cowan stopped him with a raised hand.

"We'll use my cards."

Rod dropped his unopened deck on the table and watched Cowan pull a stack of cards from a nearby drawer. Cowan dropped the pile of limp cardboards on the table. Rod laid them out by suits, handling them slowly, and verified that the stack contained a complete deck. The cards, long used, were limp, sticky, and had edges worn fuzzy.

"You feel you got to check my cards, boy?"

"You declined my cards, sir. You established the ground rule not to expect an honest deck. Now I have the right to take a look at yours."

Rod gathered the cards and riffled them in front of his eye, looking for marking. He reversed the deck and riffled them again. He took a close look at the carefully stacked deck and ran his sensitive fingers along the edges—both sides, top and bottom—to see if any cards were roughened, nicked, or trimmed. He spread the deck into a fan, then a reverse fan, then flipped the deck over and repeated the procedure. He had no intention of allowing play with cards marked with crude crimping or dog-earing. He shuffled the deck three times. Cowan leaned forward, elbows on the table, eyes fixed on Rod's hands.

"Would you like to cut, sir? Then we can draw for high card to see who deals first. What would you like to play, sir?"

Cowan answered the first question by cutting the deck. When Rod spread the deck in a fan on the center of the table, Cowan waved away cutting for high card and said, "Go ahead and deal. Five-card draw."

Rod gathered the cards. "Stakes?"

Cowan shook his head. "No money. Let's just see how good you are."

"I shall not waste your time, sir. You wanted a demonstration, and you shall get one. Who would you like to win the first hand?"

"Try to win it yourself, boy."

"Very well, sir. Consider it done."

Rod dealt four hands, dropped the deck, and laced his fingers together with his thumbs hooked over the edge of the table. "I have the four aces. Keep that in mind when you bet."

Cris said, "I don't believe you. I'll open, but just for a little bit of money." She pretended to shove a bet forward.

Milt said, "I believe him. I learned not to play cards

with him when I was only ten." He waved a hand over his cards without looking at them. "I give up." He reached over and hoisted his son from his wife's lap. A pink little hand drifted up and gripped his nose.

Cowan said, "I'll just call. Let me see them aces."

Rod said, "Nobody wants to bother drawing cards? Fine, I'll bet everything in the world." Without looking at the hand he had dealt himself, he flipped his cards face up to expose four aces and a ten.

"Well, I'll be damned—excuse me, Cris. Stacked the deck right under our noses, didn't you, son?"

Rod caught the change from "boy" to "son" and gave him a cold smile. "Of course, as you requested, sir."

"You cheat all the time, son?"

"It's seldom necessary. I don't need to arrange the cards unless I'm up against a card cheat. The best thing to do is to quit the game when I see a mechanic working the table. But I don't allow myself to lose without a battle. Thus, I stay in the game at least long enough to get back money cheated from me. Besides, I often stay in a game with a mechanic to gain practice, to sharpen my skills. It's more fun to cheat a mechanic because they really watch and know what to look out for. Most players don't understand the game well enough to keep their money out of my pocket. Cheating them simply isn't necessary."

"How did you learn to do this stuff, son?" Cowan's tone had changed.

"My father has owned and operated a pair of gaming houses since before I was born. Since I was a small child, when he caught a card sharper, or suspected one, he employed the man to show me his skills. My father also had his house men show me how they detected the cheats."

"Your old man caught card cheats and brought them home and paid them to teach his son?"

"The best ones, sir, he didn't catch. They were too clever. Their regular winnings caused him to suspect them. He offered them money to teach me, had their arms broken if they refused. I think they did it, most of them, just because the request was so unusual. The ones he caught weren't so cagey, but I still learned a lot from them. He offered no money to those he caught. He simply promised not to break their arms if they'd instruct me. A few times I had my lessons with these men with a couple of my father's armed guards in the room. Some of my instructors considered themselves dangerous men, but most of them were quite well mannered."

Rod spread four kings on the table in front of him.

Cowan leaned forward with a grin. "Now what you up to, son? Where'd them kings come from?"

"Sir, you mustn't let a card player sit with his thumbs hooked over the edge of the table like I just did. He can trap cards against the edge of the table out of sight."

Rod turned to Milt. "Take the deck and hide it under the table. Don't tell me what you're doing. Take none, one, or two cards out of the deck."

Milt, the baby's hand still gripping his nose, hid the cards for a moment. When he dropped the deck back on the table, he said, "He's going to pick up the deck now and tell you if any cards are missing."

Rod picked up the deck and shuffled them. "One card short."

Milt flipped a single card back on the table. "He could do that when we were boys. I've seen that one before." His voice, distorted by having both nostrils pinched shut, brought a giggle from Cris.

She said, "You can tell when you shuffle? Is that how you do it?"

"No," Rod answered, "that was just messing around. Do you read books, Cris?"

"Yes."

"Can you tell when you turn pages that you're turning two instead of one?"

She nodded.

"Without looking you wet a finger or something and separate the pages, don't you?"

When she nodded again, Rod asked, "You can tell you're turning two pages even though books have pages of different thickness and stiffness?"

"Yes, I can."

"That's the answer, Cris. You answered your own question. I wager that I handle decks more often than you turn pages. Books are your pleasure. Cards are my work."

Cowan said, "If I could do that kind of stuff, I'll be damned—excuse me, Cris—if I'd be working my butt to the bone—excuse me, Cris—on a cattle drive."

"When do we start?"

"We're started, son. Our main gather starts moving north tomorrow. We'll be picking up cattle along the way. I'll handle that. You and Milt got to go over to Goliad. We got men over there been gatherin' and buyin' and brandin' for a month."

Milt said, "We'll be a week or so behind Uncle Caleb, Rod. We'll head north through Waco and Fort Worth and on from there."

"Aren't you needed with your own herd?"

"Uncle Caleb and our own crew can handle that. I got a sanity problem. The drovers with your herd are mostly hired men I don't know. Being a Baynes and mildly insane, I figured to ride with you. If anything went wrong, I'd feel responsible, you see."

When Cris tittered again at his pinched-nose voice, he disengaged the little hand from his face and kissed it.

Cowan said, "He ain't worth a damn anyhow—excuse me, Cris. We don't need him. He can't throw a rope any better than you can, gambler. He's good scoutin' for water, and he's damn good—excuse me, Cris—with a gun and with noises, but he ain't the best drover in the world."

When Cris turned hard gray eyes his way and a brief silence fell, Cowan shifted his seat and rubbed his face.

Finally, reluctantly, he added, "But he's learning and that's a fact. He's learning fast. Besides, we got a damn good man—excuse me, Cris—down there for your trail boss, gambler. All you got to do is back his play, and you'll be all right."

"Who is he? What's his name?"

"Quiet little Yankee named Mill. Good man."

"Win Mill?" Rod turned to Cris.

She nodded. "Yes, Rod. Your trail boss is my brother. His cattle will be in the herd with yours."

Cowan centered his hard gaze on Rod. "Milt and Win ran into some trouble down there in Goliad a while back. Milt gave him a Navy and told him to practice with it. I hear Win wore that Navy plumb out and has got himself a brand new one now. I figured you'd want to know that, gambler. In case you get into trouble, holler for Win."

"Yes, my father told me about the trouble in Goliad. I was in Europe at the time all that happened. He came to help, but he said you had things smoothed out by the time he got here, Milt."

Milt said, "Yeah. I wrote him a letter. Uncle Rodrigo rode into town with ten or twelve armed, tough hombres behind him. That's a thing a man can't ever forget, Rod. I didn't ask him to come help. I just told him who was after me. I asked him to let my daddy and my brothers know who they might want to tend to if I couldn't get it done. Your daddy answered the call, since my folks were too far away to get here in time."

Cris broke in. "I remember your father so clearly. He and those men gave me a chill when I first saw them. Mr. Silvana looked so grim, like a vicious, utterly ruthless man. But when he greeted me he was such a warm and gentle person I felt ashamed that I misjudged him so badly."

Rod smiled. "No need for you to be ashamed, Cris. Both your impressions of my father are accurate. He can be both kinds of men you described. You're a remarkably observant woman."

He gathered the cards, shuffled them three times, and shoved them to Cowan. The old man cut the deck. "I'm going to deal each of us a hand. Watch me closely. See if you can catch me. I'm going to deal a hand to one of us from the bottom of the deck. Ready?"

The cards sailed to the exact front of each of them, sliding to a stop in four near-perfect stacks. "Now, who has the hand from the bottom?"

Cowan said, "False trail. You didn't fool me. That was an honest deal. You see any bottom dealing, Chris? Milt?"

Cris and Milt both shook their heads.

"Actually, that time I stacked the top of the deck. The only cards that came from the top went to me." Rod flipped his hand face up to reveal the four aces. "After I nullified Mr. Cowan's cut, I dealt all of your hands from the bottom, so I wouldn't disturb my top stack." He dropped the worn cards on the table and placed the unopened deck of his own on top of them. "Mr. Cowan, please accept my new deck as a small gift. I hate to see you make do with those tired old veterans. They should be retired with honors."

"Those cards marked, gambler?"

"Sir, only a complete fool carries marked cards. They provide absolute proof you are a cheat. Occasionally I trim cards and use them for practice to maintain my skill in detecting them by feel. I always practice behind locked doors, and I always burn those cards before allowing anyone to enter."

Cowan asked, "Are you quick with a gun, gambler?"

"Yes, sir, very quick. To be bested is to be dead. Isn't that true, sir?"

FIVE

THE SLIGHT FIGURE straightened into taut alertness in the saddle when Rod and Milt rode into sight. He spun his mount with easy grace and rode to meet them. Rod's stomach tightened when the rider's hand dropped to his hip. Rod knew he slipped the thong to free his holstered handgun.

"Milt, that fellow doesn't look friendly, not a bit."

"That's Win's habit. He's testy until he knows who's coming up on him. He learned caution the hard way. Fact is, I taught him a thing or two about that myself."

Halfway to them, Win recognized Milt and flashed a broad smile. Almost on top of them, he pulled his horse to a sliding stop and leaned forward to shake hands with Milt. Warmth faded from his expression when he shifted cold, appraising gray eyes to Rod. His face relaxed at Milt's first words. "Win, meet my cousin, Rod Silvana. Rod, say hello to Win Mill."

It seemed to Rod that Win hesitated for a second before turning his horse so he could grasp Rod's outstretched hand. His gaze flicked from Rod's spotless white shirt to his elegant English riding boots to the soft gloves he wore on a warm day to the ivory-handled, .36-caliber Navy riding butt forward on his left hip. Rod smiled at the transition. The man's manner slid easily and almost invisibly from cold scrutiny to habitual alertness.

"Cousin to Milt, are you?"

"Sure am."

"Yeah, he told me his middle name came from your side of the family. Rodrigo Silvana your daddy?"

"That's right."

"I met him. Your daddy came to Milt and Cris's wedding." He paused for a second as if considering his next comment. "No need to feel too bad about Milt. I'm related to him too, but just by marriage, thank God. People around here are polite and don't mention it much. My sister took a liking to him for some reason and married him, so she has to hang around with him a lot. Women do take peculiar notions sometimes. You know how they are."

Rod smiled and shook his head. "No, I really don't know much about women, but I'll take your word for it."

Milt made a halfhearted palm-up gesture toward Win and pointed a smirk toward Rod. "May I present the man everybody calls the 'quiet little Yankee.' He's trying hard to learn my style of stimulating conversation, but he's having a hard time of it."

Win continued as if Milt hadn't spoken. "I live a long day's ride away from Cowan's Fort, two days if it's hot and you don't want to kill a horse. It's a blessing. I don't have to put up with him all that much."

Win coughed, cleared his throat, and leaned away from them to spit carefully. He pulled a red bandana and wiped his face. Speaking through the cloth, he said, "Pardon me. Been spitting up mud for the last couple of days. Hanging around branding fires is the worst part of this work. I taste dust mixed with cow shit and burning hair all day long. I even eat mud in my sleep."

"You mentioned Cowan's Fort. What's that?"

At Rod's question, Win's gaze went to Milt. "You haven't told him yet?"

Milt shook his head. "Didn't seem important."

The piercing gray eyes shifted back to Rod. "That's what everybody calls Milt's ranch. The Baynes clan bought the place from Caleb Cowan, Cris and my uncle, but people around here still call it by its old name. The old man built the place like a fort and still posts guards every night. He thinks Yankees or Indians might attack any minute." Win grinned at Milt. "Unless you've changed his way of doing."

Milt asked, "You want to drop by and change that old man's mind about something? You want to try that? Be sure to let me know when you're coming. I'd hate to be off working somewhere and miss seeing that."

Win turned to Rod without answering, jerked his head toward Milt, and asked, "You got very many in your family born like him?"

"Born like what?"

"Born without a brain. Does it run in the family?"

Judas edged closer and Win reined aside sharply, spinning his horse away. "Milt, don't you put that damn crowbait up to biting me again. That isn't funny. I'll shoot him. I swear I will. Last time he got me I rubbed a sore place for a week."

Milt spoke to Rod as if Win wasn't in hearing distance. "Little redheaded Yankee's only been in Texas a few years. He still doesn't know how to handle horses worth a damn. Our vaqueros laugh at him so much when he's in the saddle he has to dismount or they can't get any work done."

"Where do you come from, Mr. Mill?"

"Kansas. Just call me Win, Rod. I guess we're kind of family in a way."

"Well, you're headed for home with this cattle drive, aren't you? That'll be pleasant for you."

Rod felt a chill when Win's eyes fixed into a cold

stare. "I left Kansas because people burned my barn and shot at my house in the night. Men I thought were my friends wouldn't even speak to me, so I came to Texas. As far as I'm concerned, Kansas is enemy country. If I see any of those people I knew back then, I might shoot on sight. My home is down near Goliad in the state of Texas. I answered your question wrong. I should have said I'm from Goliad."

"I beg your pardon. I didn't mean to touch a sore spot."

Before Win could answer, Milt said, "Forget it. All redheaded people flare up like that. You just have to let them burn off, like spilled powder. No harm in it except some heat, a little smoke, and a bad odor. You'll get used to it after a while. Being born redheaded and a runt both would spoil mighty near anybody's disposition."

Win flipped a hand toward an approaching wagon when it rounded a hill into sight. "Now what's that coming?"

Rod answered, "That's for my luggage. Milt wrote that we'd be on the trail for several months, so I brought what I thought I'd need to be comfortable."

"Brought his own man to drive it, too," Milt added, raising his head to gaze at the sky with an innocent expression. "Water barrels, extra wheel and axle, everything all loaded neat and tied down. Looks like that man of his got ready to drive to California."

Win's eyes widened. "A wagon load? You brought a wagon load of stuff?"

Rod smiled. "I like to wear clean shirts, and I like to sleep dry."

"Well," Win said doubtfully, "I guess that ought to be no trouble if you've got your own man to look after it."

"Brought his dumbbells and stuff, too." Milt added with an admiring tone.

"Dumbbells?"

"Yeah, Rod likes to get his proper exercise, make sure he keeps fit."

"Exercise?"

"Yep, that's right. He carries his exercise equipment everywhere he goes."

Win tipped his hat forward and scratched the back of his head. "Yeah, I guess lying around on a trail drive might soften a man and put fat on him if he didn't watch out." He looked at Rod. "You have a chance to talk to Caleb?"

"For nearly two days. Almost did nothing else since I got here."

Win nodded and glanced toward Milt. "I just wondered if somebody told you something to confuse you. Some folks I know have a strange sense of humor. Trailing cattle to Kansas strikes most men as tiresome. I don't think I ever heard of anybody concerned about getting enough exercise. Maybe you shouldn't mention that to any of our drovers. They might feel a bit taken down."

Rod passed a silk handkerchief around the sweatband of his hat. "It's a habit I don't ordinarily mention, but Milt asked, so I told him. I've done a lot of traveling. Got myself into habits that seem strange to some people."

"Yeah," Win said. "I understand. Around here, just mention you're related to Milt. Nothing you do will surprise people. They'll figure it comes with the bloodline. By the way, how's my nephew?"

Milt said, "Wondered how long it'd take you to ask. He's getting bigger and handsomer every day."

"Did you see him?" Win pointed the question at Rod.

"Yes, I did. Beautiful baby. Hard to tell when a youngster is still so small, but he looked like he's going to take after Milt."

Win said, "I agree, and I fear you're right. Tragic burden. Poor innocent little thing."

Milt nodded and put on the most insufferably smug look Rod had ever seen on a man. "He's old enough to tell for sure. He won't be redheaded. I can quit losing sleep worrying about that, thank heaven."

The wagon, drawn by four oxen, pulled up nearby. The driver dismounted and stretched. Rod dropped to the ground beside Win and pointed a thumb at him. "This is Win Mill, Lukie, Mrs. Baynes's brother and the trail boss on this drive. Win, meet Lukie Freeman." Win stepped down and stuck out his hand.

While the two shook hands, Rod continued, "Lukie and I grew up together. My father gave Lukie the job of looking after me when we were both babies."

Win asked, "Do you talk, Lukie?"

"Not much," Rod answered.

When Win stood waiting for him to answer for himself, Lukie glanced at Rod and drew an almost invisible nod before he spoke. "It's usually considered better manners on this side of the Atlantic for a Negro to avoid talking too much around white men, Mr. Mill. Rod speaks for me until we both agree we're among friends."

Win asked, "On this side of the Atlantic?"

"Yes, sir. I go where Rod goes, and he travels extensively. In Europe, they don't pay as much attention to my being a Negro as they do here."

"You sure don't talk like the Negroes around here." Win's comment came out like a question.

"He sat beside me when I got my tutoring," Rod said. "Just like me, he speaks French and Spanish. He also speaks illiterate Negro patois fluently if it suits him."

"Yassuh, I does. That be the truth, yassuh." Lukie snatched off his hat and bobbed his head.

Milt laughed and said, "You ought to see the look on your face, Win. Close your mouth unless you want to catch flies."

Win said, "Freeman, you ought to be on the stage. I guess I did look startled."

Rod said, "I'll ask a favor from you, Win. Milt's tickled with the idea and has already agreed."

"If Milt likes it, there must be some kind of devilment at hand. What is it?"

"Ignore Lukie. Just pay no attention to him at all. He'll

act like a sullen hired man who doesn't much like me or his job. He stays quiet and people kind of forget he's around. That lets him find out things for me now and again."

"I knew it. What'd I tell you? Just the kind of trickery that appeals to Milt. This time I like it too. I'll go along."

"If I get into trouble, Lukie's my ace in the hole. He's saved my hide more times than I can count. Sometimes we travel together. Sometimes we travel separately but to the same places. This time, since Lukie doesn't know a thing about cattle, we figured he'd better stick close to me. We couldn't think of a way he could hire on and come along otherwise."

Lukie, hat back on his head, spoke with a smile. "If trouble arises, gentlemen, you are three aces faceup. Four aces are better than three, especially if one is a hole card."

Rod said, "Milt figured my wagon could follow the cook's rig, if that's all right?"

Win merely lifted a careless hand in a palm-up gesture to indicate agreement. "Did Milt tell you I've got stock of mine with this drive?"

"Yes, I like that. It gives you a stake in the enterprise. He told me you're to be boss. I'm to keep my mouth shut unless you ask about something. I agree to that too."

Win sent an amused glance at Milt and stuck out a hand toward Rod. While they shook hands again, he said, "You got a deal. I was a little worried, having never met you. Milt said you'd act just like this. Of course, he added a sarcastic comment that I need to learn how to deal with a family full of gentlemen. We'll get along, Rod."

Rod looked at the pall of dust and smoke hanging over several branding fires in the distance. He pointed at the cook wagon upwind from the working crew. Lukie glanced at Win, got a nod, climbed aboard his wagon, and started his oxen in that direction. "I don't see nearly as many cattle as I expected, Win."

"You're only looking at a small part, that's the reason. We'll be picking up cows along the way that'll be rounded up and waiting for us, and we've got more cattle coming up from along the Rio Grande to join up with us."

"Your men bought cattle for me from that far south?"

Win glanced at Milt before he answered. "Rod, some of your cattle only understand Spanish. In fact, some of those boys we bought from were tickled to sell for only four dollars a head. They were happy to see those animals move farther north. Texans and Mexicans have a contest going down on the border."

"Contest?"

"Yeah, to see who can move the most cattle north and who can move the most south. Of course, part of the game is to do it without the other side knowing until it's too late. You see, Rod, the people who own the cattle don't enjoy the game."

Rod said, "I think I understand."

"We've still got a week of branding and notching to do on the animals we already have here. Nobody can hold a herd this size in one place more than a few days. The men move the cows every day or so to fresh grass, and they throw up a makeshift corral in a new spot so they can keep cutting out animals to brand. We'll have about thirty-five hundred head collected by the time we get north of San Antonio."

"You expect any trouble?"

Win looked away and rubbed his face. Rod guessed he covered a grin. "Nothing beyond Comanches, Apaches, Kiowas, Jayhawkers, driving rain, hail, lightning, swollen rivers, quicksand, rustlers, prairie dog holes, drought, grass fires, stampedes, buffalo, . . ."

"Never mind." Rod raised a hand to stop the litany. "Forget I asked."

"You'll meet most of the crew tonight at supper," Win said, stepping back into the saddle.

With one foot in the stirrup, Rod answered, "Good. I

might as well get over there and watch. I have a lot to learn."

The learning started the next morning. Lukie thumped Rod's tent and asked in a low voice, "You going to sleep all day?"

Rod rolled out of his blankets and searched the inky darkness for a match to light a lantern. After a breakfast of bacon and flapjacks with molasses with Milt and Win he stumbled back through inky blackness to find his tent down and already packed in Lukie's wagon. The team stood hitched and ready to go. A horse stood saddled and ready, reins tied to a wagon wheel.

Lukie smiled in the dim light of an uplifted lantern. "Cookie said he wouldn't be waiting for such as me, so I thought I'd better be ready."

"Next time, wake me up before I go to sleep. It'll save time."

Lukie chuckled and climbed into the wagon seat. "I waited until you could eat with the second shift. These people don't sleep much, boss. Midnight might as well be noon. They been riding in and out, saddling and unsaddling, drinking coffee, and whatever all night."

Milt rode by, slouched in the saddle. "Me and Win just decided you would ride with us today, Cousin. You ready?"

"I guess I'd better be." Rod grabbed the reins and swung into the brand new saddle, thankful that he'd had a couple of days to get used to it before joining the herd. The change from the familiar English design hadn't bothered him, but breaking in any new saddle gave no joy to a tender butt. The creak of new leather reminded him that he still had miles to ride before his irritated rump stopped sending painful signals.

Milt rode silently as usual while Win pointed out things he evidently wanted Rod to understand.

"The cattle go to water before first light, Rod. As soon as they've tanked up we start them walking. Now that we've got the herd on the move, you might notice that they always line out in the same order. The animals get used to being in a certain place. They get like cavalry soldiers, I guess, fitting into the column in the same position every day."

Rod nodded without reply. Then he wondered if Win could see the gesture in the darkness.

"The big white steer in front will lead this bunch all the way to Kansas. When our men riding point turn him, the whole bunch turns to follow."

At another nod from Rod, he went on, "We don't spend much time scouting water at this stage, this country being close to home. Still, 1871 has been a dry year so far, so we can't take anything for granted. Greenhorns don't understand how we can't simply drive up the same way we went last time, like driving up a road. It's not that easy. If a big herd gets ahead of us, they clean up the grass and mess up the crossings. That makes us swing off and go along a couple of miles to one side or the other if we can. Later, scouting around will get more important and more dangerous. We'll swing more to the west. Water gets scarcer and Indians more plentiful."

Rod's watch showed only half past nine in the morning when Milt spotted dust from another herd. He lifted a hand to point without saying anything. Win said, "That's some more of ours, I'll bet, right on schedule. Tell them to stop and we'll come up on 'em." Milt rode toward the dust.

Win turned his horse. "Rod, let's ride back and catch the cook."

"What happened yesterday to make the cook so testy last night?"

"Just a bad day yesterday. One of those days when everything went wrong. Had trouble getting hitched up so he got a slow start. Then he got stuck in a steep draw and had to holler for help. That embarrassed him. He doesn't like to ask the riders for a damn thing."

Win coughed and spat to the side. "Damn dust. If I had to ride drag, I wouldn't last two days." He settled himself in the saddle and went on. "Then Cookie lost a water barrel without noticing and had to go back for it. All of this bad luck made him late. By the time he got caught up, the herd had already got to the water. When the herd gets to the water first, he's got nothing but mud to work with. He likes to keep those barrels full for dry days. If you thought he was testy last night, wait till he has to cook in the rain with a high wind. We'll eat half-cooked beans, but you won't hear a word from the men."

"He seemed like a different man this morning."

"I reckon he should. Your man Lukie told him he had a spare axle in that wagon of yours. They measured it and found it would fit Cookie's wagon, too. He's been in a sweat. He cracked that axle a week ago and tied it up with rawhide. He was just hoping it would last till we got to Gonzales or somewhere to get a new one."

As they rode through a clump of trees, they saw two of their riders sitting on the ground ahead. Their horses stood ground-reined nearby. Another man stood holding a rifle on them.

"What the hell's this?" Rod asked.

Win loosened the thong over his Spencer. "Nothing for it but to go see. Looks like a homesteader. See his soddy?"

"Yeah, I do now, but I don't see why he's put a couple of our men on the ground."

"Hold back, Rod. No use in both of us riding up under that fellow's gun."

"You're the boss in front of the men, but not out here. I disagree. I'm coming with you. If that fellow wanted to hurt somebody, he'd have blasted those riders by now." Rod pulled his Navy and held it loosely across the pommel. Without further comment, they circled and separated to come in behind the rifleman, forcing him to move around the seated men to keep them in sight and dividing his attention.

Win pulled rein unexpectedly and Rod, caught by

surprise, also pulled up. The trail boss pulled his Spencer from its scabbard. For a few seconds nobody spoke. Rod could see now that the man held a shotgun rather than a rifle on the seated riders.

Win had pulled rein at the farthest edge of the shotgun's range. "What's the trouble?" He hardly raised his voice, but Rod heard him clearly and the shotgunner answered.

"These men took my cattle. Then one of them roped my dog and broke his neck. They won't ride no farther till they make it right."

One of the seated men said, "I done it, Mr. Mill. The damn dog come running up and barked his fool head off."

"You had to rope him? You couldn't run him off?"

"I'da shot the son of a bitch if I hadn't been afraid I'd set the cattle to running. We had cattle going ever' which way as it was. He wants five dollars for that crazy dog. I told him he'd have to talk to you, Mr. Mill, and we'd go get you, but he wouldn't have none of that. He said we'd just wait till you come by. We been settin' here for nearly half an hour. Hell, Mr. Mill, we got a mile-long chunk of cattle not being minded on this side of the herd. We'll be chasing bunch quitters till dark."

Win's Spencer lay in the crook of his left elbow. "Put down the shotgun, mister. You don't need it anyway. No need for anybody to die over a dog."

The man swung the muzzle away from the seated men and nestled the barrel across his chest. "I'll just hold mine like you got yours till I find out how things go here."

"Good enough." Win slid his Spencer back into its scabbard and kicked his mount forward. "You fellows get on with your work. We'll talk to this man."

The two riders wasted no time jumping into saddles, but the trail boss raised a hand to hold them in place. He dismounted and stuck out his hand to the homesteader. "I'm Win Mill."

The man stepped back, his eyes shifting to Rod. "I'm

Nello Banks. We'll shake when we get friendly. I ain't feeling friendly yet."

Now that he had come close, Rod saw that Banks could hardly be over eighteen, and he was probably younger than that. Thin as a rail, tension showed in every jerky move he made. The boy had a tense white line around his rigid lips. Rod holstered his ivory-handled Navy, eased his mount forward, and swung to the ground beside Win. He moved slowly, trying not to alarm the young man.

Win asked, "What does it take to make you feel friendly, Mr. Banks?"

"Your men cleaned me out. I only had twenty head. I figured you might buy. I need a little money real bad. Your boys just swept 'em up like they owned 'em. Then that rider killed my dog, too." He eyed Rod's white shirt and expensive riding boots. "You rich bastards come through here acting like God. What do you expect?"

Rod said quietly, "Take back that comment about rich bastards, and do it quick."

For a tense moment Rod feared Banks would swing the shotgun and force the issue, but he matched Rod's quiet tone. "I reckon I spoke out of turn there. I take that back. No cause to insult a man before I know him."

Rod turned to the two mounted men. "Did we take up cattle from this place?"

"We're always picking up strays, Mr. Silvana."

Win snapped, "That's no answer."

"I think we got some new cattle. Maybe he's telling the truth, Mr. Mill. I saw a brand I didn't remember."

Rod turned back to Banks. "Your cattle branded?"

"Damn right."

"Twenty head, you say?"

"That's right."

"Draw out your brand on the ground."

Banks drew out the brand with the muzzle of his shotgun. Rod winced inwardly to see a weapon used for a drawing stick, but the young fellow evidently didn't want to put his shotgun down to use something else. Win waved to one of the cowhands, who rode over, looked at the outline on the ground, and nodded. Win said, "You boys get back to work." When they hesitated, he added, "Go on now. We'll handle this."

Watching them depart, Win pulled a cigar and lit it. Banks eyed the smoke and licked his lips.

"You out of tobacco?"

"Yeah, for a month or so."

Win walked to his saddlebags and came back with a handful of cigars. He stuffed them neatly into his vest pocket, ends showing in an orderly row. Deliberately, he squatted on his heels and blew a long, slow stream of smoke. Rod couldn't help smiling. Watching a man wearing spurs hunker down always impressed him as an exercise in vigilant caution. Banks shifted from one foot to the other for a moment before he dropped to one knee.

"Uh, you wouldn't have one of those you could spare, would you?"

"I might, soon's things feel more friendly around here."

"I'm feeling more friendly. Sure am. That's a fact." Banks laid the shotgun on the ground beside him.

Win passed him a cigar. Banks made a show of searching his pockets until Win produced a match.

"You know how much trouble it would be to try cutting your animals out of that herd?"

"Yes, sir, but I'd consider selling. That's what I wanted to do anyhow." Banks rolled the cigar from one side of his mouth to the other, enjoying the taste.

"Twenty head, you say?"

"Yes, sir, and a damn good dog."

"And a dog." Win nodded and looked off into the distance. Banks, still on one knee, shifted uncomfortably as the silence stretched. He struck the match to light his cigar, and Rod saw his hand tremble.

"That fellow you let get behind you, his name is

Silvana," Win said in a low tone. "He's our hired gun. We use him to shoot homesteaders who raise dust."

Banks's head flew up, and he spun to meet Rod's hard gaze. He glanced sorrowfully at the shotgun lying on the ground beside him. "Well, I guess I acted the fool. I never should have shot off my mouth, and I never should have put that smokepole down. No surprise. Nothing goes my way lately."

Win blew another stream of smoke. "How about two dollars a head for those cattle of yours?"

"That'd be better than a bullet in the head, Mr. Mill, but I've heard of folks getting as much as eight here lately for prime stock."

"Yeah, for prime stock after inspection and a tally check."

"A man who'd lie about the tally would steal sheep, Mr. Mill. I wouldn't do a thing like that."

From the corner of his eye Rod saw a woman come to the doorway of the nearby sod house. She stood motionless, hands gripped together.

"Let's hear no more talk about bullets in the head, Mr. Banks. Nobody's going to get shot today. I was joshing you. Mr. Silvana is a gentleman, and he owns most of that herd passing by."

Banks took a deep breath and let it out slowly. He came to his feet and stuck out a hand. "Honored to meet you, Mr. Silvana. Since we're getting to be friendly, I might as well admit I'm out of powder too. That smokepole ain't loaded."

Win let a silence fall for a few seconds, focusing his attention on the ash of his cigar. Finally he said slowly, "I might consider four dollars. Four dollars a head for twenty head. That's a sight of money. That's eighty dollars." He shook his head like the amount was enough to buy a railroad, using the movement to conceal a wink at Rod.

"I calculate it to be a hundred and sixty dollars for the cattle, Mr. Mill. Eight dollars isn't unreasonable." Rod noticed laugh lines at the corners of the youngster's mouth for the first time. The boy had about decided he wasn't going to get shot after all. "And that doesn't count the dog."

"The dog. How could I forget the dog? What do you think, Mr. Silvana?"

Rod shook his head and said in a doubtful tone, "Nobody ever offered to sell me a dead dog before, but I'm new to Texas."

Win dug into the money pouch slung from his belt. He laid out eight twenty-dollar pieces on the ground. "Your price for the cattle. Nothing for the dog. My man felt he had to stop the dog to keep the herd from busting loose. I don't hire men who kill God's creatures for fun."

Banks fixed his eyes on the gold, licked his lips, pulled on the cigar, and thought for a moment. "I reckon that's fair." He made no move to pick up the coins.

Win picked up the money and handed it to him. "I'll need a bill of sale."

Banks nodded. "I can write, but I got no paper, Mr. Mill."

Win pulled his tally book from the inside pocket of his vest, turned a few pages, and passed it to him. Banks waited for Win to fish a stub of pencil from a shirt pocket. As soon as Banks finished writing and returned the book, Win examined it and handed it to Rod. Alerted by his straight look, Rod checked the page. The script looked like it had been written by a competent court clerk. Banks had even drawn his brand clearly and neatly. Rod looked up to find Win's brows lifted in question.

"Got some schooling, have you?" Rod asked.

"Yes, sir, but it didn't help me find work."

Rod tilted his head toward the sod house. "That your woman yonder?"

"My sister."

"Where's your pa?"

"We lost our father and mother both to fever. I couldn't

find work, so my sister and I are trying to start a ranch. We didn't have money to buy enough horses. I only had one, and he broke his leg a week ago. I couldn't even keep the cattle I rounded up from straying away. Hell, I had fifty head gathered. At eight dollars, I could have sold them for four hundred dollars. With that much money, I could make it. I thought I could keep food on the table mostly by hunting wild game, but I even ran out of powder."

Rod said, "You, sir, have more brass than a troop of cavalry. The truth is you don't know a thing about ranching."

"I know I'm a good rider. I know I can learn anything I set my mind to study. I know I got a sister to look after. I know I have to do something."

Win said, "Pack up. Mr. Silvana will send a wagon for you and your sister. Twenty-five dollars a month until we get to Abilene, Kansas. After that you're on your own. Maybe you'll learn enough to come back here and make out. At least you'll have a little money if you don't waste it."

Banks stared at Win with wide eyes for a moment. "You offering me a job?"

"That's about the size of it."

"I better ask my sister."

"That doesn't surprise me. Get to it."

The youngster came to his feet and ran toward the sod house, leaving his shotgun lying on the ground.

Rod said, "That's the dumbest thing I ever heard of, Win. Have you lost your mind? That's a green kid, and what the hell are we going to do with his sister?"

Win leaned over and stuck a fresh cigar into the muzzle of the shotgun. His stacked five others like small logs beside the trigger guard. "His sister can ride with your man Lukie. He'll look after her. You can move out so she can sleep in your tent. I admire a kid with enough guts to face armed men with an empty shotgun. We can use another rider, green or not, and that kid's desperate enough to make a good hand. You can say thank you now."

"I can say what?"

"Thank you."

"What on earth for?"

"For me taking that kid on. This way I take the blame if it doesn't work out. You were going to do it. You were melting like butter in the sun."

"Nonsense."

"I could see you thinking abut it. You were thinking that the first stray Comanche to come drifting through here would ride away with two easy scalps."

"The hell I was. I don't know a thing abut Comanches."

"It was written all over your face. You must wear a mask when you play cards—I never saw such a sad face. I had to make the offer before you burst out in tears. You'd have offered that kid a hundred a month."

Banks came running out of the soddy. He shouted, "Sis says we'll be ready by the time your wagon gets here."

Rod and Win mounted and rode silently for fifteen minutes. Rod spoke first. "You're not so damn smart. I was only going to offer thirty a month."

Win's shout of laughter startled his horse into a string of crow hops and Rod's into a skittish gallop.

Win fell silent on the ride back, and Rod had plenty of time to think. His face had given him away, and he didn't like that. Win had read his sympathy for young Nello Banks and had solved the problem, but he had solved it in a way that left Rod in tight-lipped anger. In fact, the more he thought about it the more it upset him.

He treasured his privacy. He needed a quiet place away from prying eyes. His habits had become a calming ceremonial, a ritual of card practice and physical exercise that would astonish and amuse these untutored riders no end. Through all his travels, his routine had always given him a sense of security, offset the strangeness of new environs, and bolstered his confidence that constant practice kept his skills finely honed.

Win, without hesitation, had given away both Rod's wagon and his tent. As trail boss, he had no right to give away Rod's property so casually. Well, he hadn't exactly given them away, but he had robbed Rod of their use. Now he faced the prospect of sleeping in the rain just like the hired men, if it ever rained in this dry country. A proper owner always kept a distance from employees, stayed aloof from their petty problems. With a woman in his wagon, he'd have to ask permission to have access to his own clothing. No, he wouldn't do that. He'd get Lukie to do that for him.

This discomfort didn't have to last long. He'd arrange to drop the woman off somewhere. Surely they would pass some town where she could be left in a safe place. Rod could pay her food and rent if young Nello Banks didn't see his way clear to do it. It could be put down to the cost of doing business. Shouldn't cost much anyway. A poor orphan girl probably wouldn't expect much.

No, Rod would pay the expense out of his own money belt. His father could pick out an odd item on an expense list as easily as a hound could find a bone in the dark. Rod couldn't imagine how he'd explain such an expenditure in the face of his father's humorless questioning.

"You picked up a young orphan girl?" Rodrigo would ask. His tone would be the same as if he'd asked, "You got drunk, shaved your head, and danced naked on an anthill?"

"Yes, sir," he could imagine himself answering.

"You did this without even having met the woman?"

"Yes, sir."

"And your purpose behind this remarkable decision?"

Rod could imagine a thundering silence.

"I felt sorry for her and her brother, sir."

"You . . . felt . . . sorry? The contempt he could predict in his father's voice caused Rod's face to burn.

He forced himself to stop engaging in ridiculous fantasy. His father must never learn of this breach of judgment.

Whoever heard of taking a woman on a trail drive? Damned if he knew. He'd never thought to ask, but the idea seemed outlandish. The average age of Win's riders probably came to less than twenty. The potential of her causing trouble was simply too great to be tolerated, even if she were the sort to behave properly. Paying a bit to be rid of her could be compared to buying insurance. It made sense. God forbid, though, that Rodrigo Silvana should hear of the matter.

If Rodrigo were to hear about this unfortunate incident in some way, Rod could shift the blame. Win had given him an escape route, and the clever fellow had even said so. He could tell Rodrigo the decision came from the local manager. While not the whole truth, at least that wouldn't be a lie. The prospect of telling an outright lie to Rodrigo Silvana would give any man with an ounce of brains reason to pause.

Rod could claim he had corrected the error in the quickest and most honorable manner he could. In fact, he had disapproved so strongly, he could tell his father, that he'd paid the expense from his own funds. No reason to admit to his father that he'd been "melting like butter in the sun."

SIX

LUKIE'S EXPRESSION REVEALED nothing. He rubbed his mouth and turned on the wagon seat to stare in the direction Rod pointed. "Over yonder a bit, in that direction, you say?"

"Yeah, young fellow named Nello Banks and his sister. I don't know his sister's name. He said his only horse broke a leg a few days ago."

"I guess the sister can ride with me. Want me to take a horse for Mr. Nello Banks?"

Rod clapped his hands together in fake applause, his eyes wide with mock surprise. "Good idea, I'm glad you thought of that."

Lukie's eyes rolled, and he took a deep breath. "He does have his own saddle, I suppose?"

"If he doesn't, he rides bareback."

"I hope they don't bring much. This wagon isn't exactly full of empty."

"Banks looked poor as a field mouse. I doubt they'll have much." Rod leaned from the saddle to put his face close to Lukie's. "Besides, it's a soft job for you to make room. Just throw out some of your money."

Lukie's expression brightened and he tapped his temple. "Yeah, that ought to do it. It's a good thing I thought of that." He snapped the reins and put his wagon into motion.

Rod wanted to distance himself as much as he could from Nello Banks and his predictably pitiful sister. He spent the remainder of the daylight hours drifting along watching the riders control the moving cattle. He had already learned to ride on the western side of the herd if he had a choice. The prevailing wind from the southwest rolled dust into the face of any rider on the eastern side, and the incredible heat produced by the mass of moving animals astonished him. Had anyone tried to tell him that drovers' faces would be reddened by heat from a cattle herd like men who spent too much time near a hot stove, he would have scoffed. Now, he wasn't so sure.

The sun sank low and Rod shifted once again in his futile attempt to find a less sore place on his rear, when the sound from the herd changed in the blink of an eye. The pace of the slowly moving animals jumped from a forward amble into a gallop. The awesome pound of hooves shook the leaves on a clump of nearby trees into what looked like fearful tremors. In an instant, as if the herd of animals were all of one mind, every beast leaped from a sedate shamble into a wall-eyed run. Rod saw no change in the direction of the herd, and the flank riders he could see showed no reaction except to increase the speed of their mounts and to sit straighter in their saddles.

Caleb Cowan had told him about this. "Nothing can stop Texas critters if they decide to run," he'd said. "Drovers can turn 'em, maybe, but if they decide to run, they're going to run. Sometimes, they decide to stampede in the right direction. That ain't too bad if they don't run into a thicket and split up into a hundred different directions. Mostly, they run the wrong way, and that can be bad as hell. All the drovers can do is stay with 'em and try to hold the herd together.

"Why do they stampede? Hell, son, sometimes there's a reason we can figure. A bear pees upwind, a mountain lion screams, a drover strikes a match to light a cigar just like he's done a thousand times before, the cook drops a tin plate, or whatever. Most likely, they'll decide to run from thunder and lightning, but when you expect 'em to, they likely won't. Daytime, nighttime, it makes no mind. Sometimes, they run just for the stupid hell of it. I swear they do. Usually, the smart thing to do is just go with 'em. If they run toward trouble, toward bad country, try to turn the leaders and let 'em run in a circle till they get tired of front parts chasing hind parts. They ain't smart, you know."

Rod started when Milt spoke. "First stampede you've seen?"

"Where did you come from?"

"Behind you. You were so interested in watching the cattle and contemplating, you didn't keep your eyes and ears open. Bad habit."

"I'll remember that. Yeah, this is the first time I've seen a stampede. Cowan told me about it."

"Nothing to this one. Nice. They're already tired, so they won't go far. They won't even run through the cook's camp. They're going the right direction and sticking together. Sometimes, if they run into broken country, we have to spend a week gathering them up again if we can find them. I hate it when they stampede back the way we just came. That means we have to gather them and drive back over ground we already covered."

"Do you know what started it?"

"No telling. Makes no difference. Lucky for you to see a little run like this one. No harm done, just a lot of dust kicked up. You'll be more ready for it when we have a bad one."

"Ready for what?"

"Ready to keep a good night horse saddled and ready. Simple stuff like that. Being caught on foot in front of a stampede at night is a Texan's idea of sloppy thinking. Being told something doesn't impress it on the mind like seeing the need for yourself. If they run at you, don't try to be a drover. Act like a rich owner. Get on your horse and run like hell."

"Seems like I ought to be doing something to help."

Milt casually looked away to scan his surroundings, a movement so familiar Rod hardly noticed it anymore. "You're the owner, a gambler in a white shirt. The boys already tagged you for a greenhorn who isn't sure which end of a steer grows horns. They call you Blind Shuffle. You move slow and keep your mouth shut, just feeling your way along. They figure you to be smart. You don't know yet how to read the cards in a new game, so they respect you for holding back and staying out of the way. Win got a good cook, forked over money to gather up a stock of decent food, and bought good horses, so the men figure you to be square, no cheating on expenses to milk profit from the crew."

"What do they call you, Milt?"

"They call me Mr. Baynes." Milt turned in his saddle to scan ground behind him, but Rod caught his sour smile. "Most of these drovers are still just young boys, and my family has a gunpowder reputation, Rod. You know that. They'll probably call you Mr. Silvana after you shoot somebody. About half of them claim they've already done that themselves, you know. Just talk, I figure, about as truthful as how many girls they say have fallen for them." He nudged his horse into motion. "Let's go find the chuck wagon. I'd like to be first in line for a change."

Rod walked his horse beside Milt's in silence for a while before he asked, "You spend about as much time looking behind as ahead. Why? You afraid somebody will creep up on you?"

"I help Win find water, so I always ride ahead to look

things over. If we're headed toward any kind of trouble,
I try to give warning. That's harder to do with an arrow
or a bullet in my back. Besides, nobody thinks it's funny
when a scout goes out and gets himself lost. Country
looks different depending on what direction you go. I
look back, see what things look like. Then, when I want
to ride back toward where I came from, things look
familiar. I know my way."

"Simple."

Milt chuckled when Rod turned to look back. "Sure.
Nothing to it. Everything's simple once you understand
it. All a man needs is practice and enough sense to stay
awake. Having somebody to tell you things gives an
advantage if a man listens. I notice you listen just fine."

"Win picked up a new rider today, Milt."

"I know."

"How did you know?"

"My Indian nose."

"Your what?"

"My Indian nose. I can smell a poorly guarded horse
or woman from miles away. I saw those goings-on with
my binoculars. I didn't want to shoot that kid, so I was
doing some figuring about what to do when you and Win
rode up big and grand. Sometimes riding right straight at
it isn't the smartest way to handle a snag, Cousin Rod."

Rod sat straighter in the saddle. He knew for a
certainty that the mild tone of reproof, rare for Milt,
turned a casual remark into a serious lesson. "What
would you have done if that kid started trouble?"

"I'd have killed him." Milt hawked and spat. "Would
have been a shame, but pulling guns on my kinfolks
makes me short on patience with people. Sometimes you
can avoid a shooting if you don't come straight at a man
when he's drawn a line and planted his feet." He pointed
at the chuck wagon halted in a swale under a cluster of
live oaks. "I shot two turkeys this morning, nice big
birds. Cook's making stew. Chops everything all up and
throws it in a big pot after pulling out the bones. Cooks

quicker and keeps hungry riders from fist-fighting over favorite pieces. We want to be early."

"We got a visitor? I see another wagon in camp."

"That's the second wagon to carry food and gear. It just met us today, and it's loaded to the canvas. We got a big crew here, Rod. We have open spaces later on. We'll ride for days and days without seeing a house, without seeing anything but empty country."

"Good. You and Win seem to have thought of everything. Did you see the boy's sister?"

"She stayed out of sight." Milt took a deep breath and let it out slowly. "The boy's boots are worn to shreds and patches. The sister leaves a barefoot print." His final comment came just before they dismounted. "Her print's narrow. She grew up wearing shoes."

"How did you know it was her print, not one of his?"

Milt yawned. "Woman's print is usually narrower at the heel, wider at the toes. Besides, her print was way too small to fit the boy."

Win walked to meet them. "No cattle lost today, Mr. Silvana. We have a tired herd, so tonight should be quiet."

"That's good." Rod stopped his mount and swung to the ground. Win didn't turn to accompany them to the fire. His motionless stance indicated he had more to say. The men gathered around the chuck wagon stopped moving and made no effort to conceal their interest.

"We had a couple of new calves dropped today. I wonder if you could carry them on your wagon for a couple of days till they get strong enough to follow their mamas?"

"Are those calves worth anything?"

"No. The buyers just ignore them when we get to Kansas. They're still too little to make much meat."

"What's the point then? Cowan said it's common practice to kill them and keep moving."

Win spoke gravely and louder than was his habit. "That's right, but the riders hate that. They don't like to kill baby calves. They call it killing innocents. I don't like it either. Your man and Miss Banks could look after them. Their mamas will trail along behind the wagon. We could drive the mamas off, but they'd just come right back. We'll need the mama cows to feed the young'uns anyway."

"Doesn't sound very sensible. Sounds like a lot of trouble for no profit."

"That's right. It'll be inconvenient, and I guess it doesn't make much sense."

"All right, that's plain enough." The stillness made it clear that every man in the camp waited for Rod's answer. "Do it anyway."

Instantly the rustle of movement and murmur of conversation resumed. Rod wondered if he imagined the whole crew had been holding its breath.

Win said in a low voice, "Dumb decision, Mr. Silvana, but sometimes it's smart to do something dumb. Sorry to put you under the gun with no warning, but that's the way it had to happen. These ignorant Texans like to work for a tough man, but he has to have a heart. I had to tell them I couldn't throw calves on your wagon without asking."

"But you can throw Nello Banks's sister on my wagon without asking. What the hell's the difference?"

Win rubbed his chin and chuckled. "Well, for one thing, in Texas we don't shoot sisters and leave them behind when they're inconvenient and not worth a profit."

Rod nodded solemnly. "That's an interesting cultural insight. So now I guess you're one of these ignorant Texans too?"

"Sure am." Win's smile flashed in the thickening darkness.

Milt's remark came from the nearby darkness along with exaggerated lip smacking. "Both of you are ignorant. You better fill plates before all the good part's gone."

Rod lowered his voice. "Win, buy another wagon and hire another man to drive it. I don't mind you doing something like this to keep the men happy, but for heaven's sake, stop using my rig for a place to throw everything helpless you come across."

"No need to hire another man, Mr. Silvana." Rod could only catch a dim outline of the speaker in the poor light. "I'll drive the new wagon and look after the helpless babies decent men don't want to kill or leave behind."

The unexpected sound of a cultured woman's voice caused Rod to jerk his head in a double take in her direction, a startled gesture he instantly regretted. The gambler in him deplored any unplanned move. He tried to cover the slip by sweeping off his hat.

Win spoke quickly. "Miss Banks, may I present Mr. Silvana."

She approached as Rod bowed, his hat still in his hand. Her bonnet concealed her features. Other than that she stood nearly as tall as her lanky brother, Rod could tell nothing of her appearance. She sounded mature, nothing girlish in her voice.

"You heard an unguarded, jesting comment, Miss Banks. I would not have you take offense at my foolish sense of humor. I apologize."

"No need, Mr. Silvana. I wanted to take the first opportunity to thank you for giving my brother employment. We've been having a hard time. Also, I want to thank you for simply giving me a safe place to be. I'll make myself useful. You won't regret your kindness."

"Well, that's most gracious of you, Miss Banks, but I don't think you should plan to stay with us long. You see, . . ."

"I can drive the wagon with the little calves until they're strong enough to follow their mothers. I can help the cook. He really needs more assistance preparing food for this many men. As we go along, I can find other ways

to help. If any of your men get sick, I can look after them
so your drovers won't be bothered."

Rod hated the darkness. He gauged men's intentions
by careful attention to fleeting facial expressions. Women
were often more difficult, but this situation gave him no
chance at all. Her face, hidden from the flickering light in
the shadow of her bonnet, might as well be concealed by
a mask. Again, the camp fell into silence so every man
could hear every word. Rod felt like a performer on a
stage.

Trail customs remained a mystery, even though Caleb
Cowan and Win Mill tried to pour as much information
into him as they could. Neither of them had mentioned
the possibility of women being involved. Cowan had
compared the men on a trail to a pirate crew. Suppose the
men thought women attracted bad luck, like the old
seamen's superstition. Rod felt trapped. If he denied her
request, he might alienate a callow bunch of drovers,
every one of them seeing himself as a Sir Galahad and
God's gift to women. No telling what they might do. If he
accepted, no telling what kind of trouble might result.

He decided to fall back on the weakest ploy of all.
When in doubt, delay. "For the moment, make yourself at
home, Miss Banks. I think we should try to find a better
and safer place for you than with a trail herd, but we can
discuss this later. It's the end of a long day, and I'm
tired."

"Of course, Mr. Silvana. I put out your bowl of water
and your towel beside your tent so you can wash up. I'll
bring your plate to you." She moved away before he
could respond.

Rod hesitated, idly slapping his hat against his leg
while he rubbed the stubble on his chin. Milt walked up
close, his tin plate already empty. He whispered, "Did
you feel the hook, little fish? I think the lady just signed
on to look after you during this dreadful trail ride.
Grateful little thing, isn't she?" He walked away with a
derisive chuckle.

Rod walked to his tent. By the light of a lantern hung at the entrance he saw his bedroll laid out inside. She stood beside a tin bowl of water, holding one of his towels. Not knowing what else to do, he rinsed his hands and face and blindly accepted the towel. He spoke through the cloth. "Thank you, Miss Banks. Look, you don't need to—"

Before he could finish, she said, "I'll fill your plate and bring it right over." She turned and walked away, leaving him with his hand lifted in a futile gesture to stop her. Feeling the fool, he glanced around. Lukie, in the shadows of his nearby wagon, minced and fluttered around in his imitation of a rich, spoiled, effeminate Parisian fop.

Rod pointed at him and said in a low, harsh voice, "Watch it, you half-wit. I haven't shot a man all day."

Lukie waggled powerful hands on limp wrists in a parody of fear, then spoke frankly. "You be good to that woman. I've decided I like her. She's smart enough to ask good questions, knows how to get things done, and doesn't waste time. She's quicker to make herself useful than any other white woman I ever saw."

"Have you been telling her what to do?"

"You gave me the job to look after her, didn't you? I've just been answering questions, that's all. What else can a poor little ex-slave do when a white woman asks him things?"

"With friends like you, I need to run to my enemies for help."

"She's coming back. Eat your dinner. We'll talk later. I got some things to tell you."

She approached with the free, confident stride of a strong walker and placed his tin plate on the box close to the lantern. "I asked the cook earlier if he saved food back for you, and he said he did, so he was expecting me. It's nice not to have to stand in line."

"Yes, I suppose so. Miss Banks, have you eaten?"

"Oh, yes."

"Well, that's nice."

Both hands leaped to her face. She had finally caught his reluctance to sit on the ready camp stool while she still stood. "Oh, my goodness, where is my mind?" She darted to his tent and came back with Lukie's stool. She settled herself on it, leaning forward as if ready to spring up instantly. Rod noted that she smoothed her skirt expertly. He couldn't see her feet, but her gliding movement convinced him Milt was right. She wore no shoes.

"Please relax, Miss Banks. I must thank you for your generous attentions, but—"

"You deserve a little attention. Lukie told me you spend every day and half of every night in the saddle. He said you work harder than any of your men."

"I see. Well now, about the things Lukie might have told you, . . ."

"He's such an unusual man. I don't believe I ever spoke to a Negro man before. He said you saw to it that he got the same education you did, but he made me promise not to talk to the other men about it. It might make them jealous for a Negro to have such advantages."

"Yes, well, he's unusual all right. He—"

"He's so helpful. He knows exactly how you like things. That's how I knew what to do. He explained everything and said he'd help if I had any questions. That way I wouldn't have to bother you."

Rod decided he would never finish a comment in this woman's presence unless he blurted it out so fast she'd have no chance to interrupt. She perched on Lukie's stool, tense as a frightened bird, crouched and ready to spring into flight.

"I'm sure you'd never be a bother, Miss Banks. Your pardon, ma'am, but I'd like to ask a small favor, if you wouldn't think me forward."

"You have but to ask, Mr. Silvana."

He cleared his throat. "It's just that I find it a bit strange talking like this. I haven't had the pleasure . . .

that is, now the sun is down and can't burn you . . . uh, what I'm trying to say is I can't see your face. Would you mind, Miss Banks, removing your bonnet?" Rod felt like a muttering, incoherent fool. Expecting to be interrupted every second caused him to speak like a stuttering, confused oaf.

She pulled the end of the ribbon to loosen the knot, slipped off the bonnet, and settled it in her lap.

Rod dropped his fork.

SEVEN

QUICK AS A hungry cat, she snatched the fork away before his groping hand came near it. "I'll rinse this off and bring it right back." Before he could say a word, she strode off, leaving him with a hand still suspended six inches from the ground.

Rod straightened and spoke quietly, knowing Lukie always found a way to hear anything that interested him. "Did you see that?"

Lukie spoke from the darkness under the nearby wagon. "I told you. Nothing slow about that one, mind or body. If she's that quick with a gun, we better hope she has a forgiving nature."

"Never mind that foolishness, you blabbermouth. What's all this about me insisting you get the same education I did? Have you started hitting the bottle? You been shooting off your mouth about my whole history to that woman. Besides, that was my father's doing, not mine."

"You forget things, Rod. About the time we were ten,

77

your father figured I could be more useful doing other things. You sat like a post, staring at the wall like a simpleton, and refused to speak or touch your lessons unless I came back. I guess you forgot all that."

"Oh, well, I just needed somebody around who was dumber than I was to slow things down. Never mind that. What's got into you anyhow? All of a sudden you're acting the fool. I guess it proves the point."

"What point?"

"Give a fool some schooling and you end up with a man who can use big words to say foolish things. We'll play hell using you for an ace in the hole if you spill your guts to everybody."

"She's not everybody."

"Maybe. Maybe not. How do you know she doesn't spill everything she knows? By heaven, she caught me by surprise, nearly knocked me over. I had no idea she might look like that. Who could have expected such a thing? I think she's going to be bad luck for us, Lukie. An ordinary girl would be more than enough extra trouble around all these woman-hungry drovers. A clock-stopping, raving beauty is going to be a boil on both cheeks of our butts. She looks like trouble with both barrels loaded. Every day one of these idiots is going to try to shoot somebody to defend her honor and be a hero."

"Maybe. So far all they've done is wear out razor strops and scrape faces. The cussing dropped off to nothing but whispers and mumbles, too. Seems to me like everybody's all sweetness and good behavior."

"You have to break your back loading the wagon?"

"Lord no, Rod. I don't think they had much of anything to bring. She only brought a little batch of stuff wrapped in a couple of blankets. Didn't even have a carpetbag. I asked if that was all, and she said they didn't want to be a burden. I wonder if that Banks boy has an extra shirt. She asked me how best to go about asking you to let her go to Kansas with us. Said it would cost too

much for her brother to leave her somewhere along the
way. Said they needed to save every penny."

"So? What did you tell her?"

"I told her to do exactly what she's doing. She caught
on quick, didn't she? Got you on the run from the starting
gun. Hey, did you hear that rhyme?"

"You son of a bitch. Now I'm about to get really mad.
Did you actually advise her how to cause me trouble?"

"Sure did. Quick, isn't she? Not only that, she's not
pushy. Flat refused to take our tent. Said she could make
a little bed for herself in the wagon. Seemed better and
safer to me. I told her that was a smart move, knowing
you wouldn't put up with being uncomfortable for long.
You'll be happy with this deal if you'll think about it."

"That's just great. Now I'm too delicate to stand the
slightest discomfort. I think I'll shoot you as soon as I
catch you in a good light. Thanks. Thanks a lot."

"*De nada,* you're welcome, and *il n'y a pas de quoi.*
You're really upset about this, aren't you?"

"How in the world could you tell? Was is something I
said? How crude of me."

Lukie dropped his voice to a whisper. "Watch it. Here
she comes."

Rod came to his feet when she drew near, accepted his
fork with a mumbled thanks, watched her take her seat,
and sank back down on his own stool. He intended to put
a stop to this little problem right now, but she spoke
while he was still picking the right words.

"Lukie told me you weren't a real cattleman, but I
would have guessed that anyway."

"Oh, he did, did he?"

"You being dressed up fancy doesn't matter. No telling
what a cattleman might wear. But you take off your hat
when you sit down to eat. Texans never do that outdoors
and seldom indoors."

She plucked his hat off the ground and began to brush
off the dust. Stunned, Rod recognized his wire brush in
her hand. That cursed Lukie! He must have led her

through Rod's belongings, must have shown her everything he owned. Lukie, the vigilant guard of his privacy, had opened his trunks for her, no question about it. Only Lukie and Rod had keys. He sat very still, holding his tongue until he got past feeling so aggravated.

She went on, speaking with quiet authority. "With your soft complexion, you shouldn't take your hat off either. The sun will make you sick. A serious sunburn can give you a fever. Are you left-handed?"

The quick shift of subject made him hesitate. He used that technique himself sometimes when trying to trick someone into an unguarded response. He answered carefully. "No, ma'am. Why do you ask?" Soft complexion, indeed. He wondered if she thought he should take naps like a child.

"You eat with your left hand."

"That's the way I was taught. That's the way they do it in Europe."

"Oh, you're from Europe? You talk like an American."

"I'm from New Orleans, Miss Banks. I've traveled extensively in Europe on business."

Rod fought off the temptation to go turn down the wick on the lantern. Hardened, indeed challenged, by acute observation at the gaming tables, Rod found this woman's rapt, unblinking stare rattled him. A little darkness would come in handy. For God's sake, the woman had probably even been poking around in his dirty underwear.

He cut his food in small bites, fearful he'd dribble bits down his shirt front. When he realized what he was doing, a gloomy shock snapped through him. A gambler who lost confidence in the steadiness of his hands inspired nothing but pity.

A glance downward told him the worst. His shirt, coated with dust, showed as many specks as a thrush's breast. A man forced to eat with globs of sweat-mud crusted on a filthy shirt didn't deserve such unrelenting inspection. Dressed fancy, was he? Ridiculous. He had never sat down for a meal in a more filthy condition in his life. Had he caught a trace of sarcasm? No. Her tone dripped admiration.

He searched his mind for tactful, gentle words to tell her to go away, to leave him alone, to stop watching him like a hawk, to stop violating his privacy. He'd never had to tell a woman such a thing. Always before, he could simply excuse himself and walk away.

Rod extended both hands toward her, a signal he'd seen stage actors use to quiet applause so they might speak. "Look, Miss Banks, I thing we need to reach an understanding. I suggest——"

"Oh, don't concern yourself, Mr. Silvana. Lukie said he'd tell me everything I need to know. He said not to bother you, that it was inefficient for you to be tending to little personal things when you needed all you time to look after your men and cattle. He said people would resent having the president of the United States spend time shining his own shoes when the country needed looking after. Every important man needs someone to look after the little things for him, so he can give his full attention to the big things. That's smart, isn't it?"

Rod made himself breathe smoothly and relax. Nothing worked. This woman could not be stopped. For the first time in his life, Rod wanted to leap to his feet and shout, "Shut up! Shut up and let me finish!" His measured, pedantic manner of speech worked perfectly at the gaming tables. With her, it simply gave her chances to beat him out of an opportunity to speak. When confidence returned that he could fake a pleasant tone of voice, he said, "I suppose so. Yes, I guess Lukie's a very clever fellow."

Lukie's mouth must have run at top speed all afternoon. Evidently Lukie had found a way to finish a sentence without this woman cutting him off. Too tense to eat, Rod put down his fork.

"Are you finished?"

"Yes, thank you." He rose to go wash his plate,

thinking he could grab a moment to think without enduring her unblinking observation.

"Here, I'll do that for you." She grasped his plate, and Rod forced himself to release it. He'd be fried in hell before he'd get into a tug of war with this worrisome woman over a damn soiled plate. The pleasant thought came to him that maybe he could wash up a bit and hide in his blankets before she could clean the plate and get back.

"Are you sure you had enough? You didn't eat much."

"Yes, thank you."

She took his eating utensils and trotted away.

"Lukie?"

"I'm still here."

"First she's afraid I'll get sunburned. Now she's deciding whether or not I eat enough. This is insufferable. That woman will put me in an asylum if this keeps up. I can't tell her a damn thing without her jumping in with some kind of wisdom from Brainy Black Lukie the Negro Oracle of the West."

"She sure follows instructions, doesn't forget one thing."

Rod took another long, deep breath and reminded himself again to relax. "All right. I don't know what you're up to, Lukie, but I don't like it. I'm going to put this down to a poor effort to be funny. A joke's a joke. Call her off and I'll forget it. I can be a good sport. Otherwise, I'll kill you first thing in the morning."

"Can't."

"Don't tell me that. I won't hear it. Not for a minute."

"Listen, Rod. That's a proud lady. She wants to work for her beans, won't take charity. She'd doing what I told her she needs to do if she wants to stick with this drive. She's doing things I do for you all the time. Let her. I need to tend to some other things. We have a couple of men on this drive I think need watching. You got to turn me loose so I can work. You hear me?"

Rod caught himself tapping the box in front of him

with a finger, an indication of taut nerves, loss of control. He stopped instantly and clasped his hands together. The camp grew quiet as the first shift of night herders rode out and the other men sought their blankets.

"Rod, you got to decide."

"All right. I'll go along for a little while. I don't spend much time around the camp anyway."

"Good. Not many men have the strength of character to bear the burden you're taking on, Rod. At great sacrifice, the mighty man consents to allow a beautiful woman to wait on him hand and foot. Of such come the stories of song and legend."

"Lukie?"

"What?"

"You tell her something for me. I can't tell her a damn thing."

"What?"

"You tell, her, if she interrupts me one more time, I'm going to get a rope and drag you through cactus."

"Good night, Rod."

"*Hasta mañana,* Lukie. I still think she's going to be bad luck."

Rod stepped into his tent, glanced at the clean shirt and socks laid out ready for tomorrow, and wondered if Lukie or the Banks woman had done it. His washbasin sat ready on a small folding table, flanked by a washcloth and towel. Lukie knew that even if Rod cleaned up for dinner, he often did exercises before retiring, and he hated to allow sweat to sour on him overnight.

He glanced at the light dumbbells and decided against it. He hesitated when his gaze fell on a pair of new decks of cards before deciding to skip his usual practice session too. He went through a few perfunctory stretching exercises, put out the lantern, and sank down onto his blankets. His back and legs continued to ache from sixteen hours in the saddle. Disgusted and embarrassed, he shifted around to ease his irritated rear and found the soreness evenly distributed. His tortured ass felt sand-

blasted. Tomorrow he planned to spend a couple or three
hours walking beside his horse. That should loosen him
up, maybe, and give his poor butt a rest.

Rod felt his eyes had only closed for a few minutes
when the racket of a plunging horse and Win's shout
woke him. "They're running again, boys!"

He rolled off his blanket and, following a newly
learned habit, shook out his boots before he jerked them
on, not taking time for his socks. By the time he found
his way to his staked night horse in the darkness and
tightened the saddle cinch, the hoofbeats of departing
drovers told him he was slow.

Fear came over Rod in a wave. The terrified blatting of
the running herd, thundering hoofbeats, and near-total
darkness stiffened him in the saddle. He kicked his
mount to a gallop, hardly able to see his hand in front of
his face, knowing that when he came up with the herd he
didn't have any idea what he should do.

Turn them, that's what Cowan had said. Which way?
Maybe it didn't matter. Turn them so they would mill, so
they would run in a circle until control could be regained.
Even if he could do that, which way would be best?
Suppose he turned them back toward the camp? The
cook could be killed and the remuda scattered.

He didn't know where the camp was anymore. His
horse turned under him every few jumps to avoid brush
in the darkness. Thank God, Win or somebody had
selected a good night horse for him. He congratulated
himself for having the courage to ride with a loose rein,
giving his horse freedom to pick its own way. It was
common talk among the drovers that horses could see in
the night, but some could see better than others. He eased
back on the reins. If he planned to be any help to
anybody, he'd better not break his neck and he'd need a
horse under him with something left.

Rod felt he rode as well as anybody, but he'd never
ridden at a tearing run in a black night through unknown
country. He decided, if he lived, he'd buy sugar at the

next town and pay more attention to the horse between his legs. He couldn't even remember the animal's color or its name. Every horse in the remuda had a name, but he hadn't paid attention.

He muttered through clenched teeth, "Horse, get me through this night and I'll give you sugar every day. Every damn day, you hear me?" With only a split second's bunching of muscle to give warning, the horse leaped an invisible gully, and Rod came within an inch of losing the saddle. He yelled, "Twice a day, damn you, twice a day." He laughed into the night at himself. The absurdity of trying to bargain with a dumb beast pushed back the cold hand of fear, and he began to ride more confidently.

Guided only by noise and the smell of dust, Rod tried to angle his mount toward what he guessed to be the front of the herd. One moment he rode alone. The next instant, the rolling rumble of cattle closed around him, and he blinked and narrowed his eyes. Before he could have snapped his fingers he passed from clean air into a blizzard of stinging sand, dust, and chunks of dirt pelting him like hail. He felt the horse under him flatten into a sprint, and the packed cattle thinned. He rode in front now, the surging wall of horns only a few jumps behind.

Somebody yelled, "Turn 'em to the right, to the right!"

Rod saw a flicker of a swinging movement from a shadowy rider ahead and guessed the man was swinging a slicker or a blanket. The rider shouted again. "I can't turn 'em by myself! Git up here and help me!" Then the shadow went down. Even over the pounding of the herd, Rod heard the despairing cry of the rider and the sickening crash as horse and rider hit the ground. Without thinking, without daring to draw rein, Rod leaned and swung his right arm toward a flicker of movement in the darkness. The crushing collision nearly ripped him from the saddle, and the horse under him staggered and nearly went down.

Somehow, the lithe rider got himself up behind Rod

and groaned in a cracked voice, almost a sob, "Run! Run, if you don't want a horn up your butt." Then he shouted in Rod's ear, "Shoot by that sombitch right there. Shoot right by that big bastard's ear. Shoot! Quick!"

Rod pulled his Navy and emptied it almost in the face of a huge steer now running beside them, six-foot horns nearly touching his leg. The next shout in his ear was, "He's turning, by God. Keep pushing him. Keep pushing."

Rod kept crowding the big steer, and the puncher reached forward and grabbed Rod's rope, a rope he carried but never used. Swinging the coiled rope at the steer's flank, the puncher kept the steer turning to the right, and the animals behind followed.

Then they were running straight at a stream of cattle crossing their route. The puncher behind him shouted, "We done it. Now git us out of the way. Pull away! Don't get amongst 'em. The other boys can finish this. Rein off yonder to the left. This horse is gonna come unwound any minute carrying double." The man's voice lost its frantic tone. His next comment came with a laugh. "Get our ass out of the way before God loses interest and tends to somebody else."

Seconds later they rode in what seemed eerie quiet, yet the pounding, horn-clattering herd continued to crash past less than a hundred yards away.

The man said, "Let me down a minute. I'm hurtin' all over. Let me catch my breath." When Rod reined in, the man slid off the rump of the horse and knelt. Rod swung down and started to speak when something about the man's stillness stopped him. He realized, almost too late in the darkness, that he should keep quiet, that the drover's posture was that of a man in prayer. Caught by surprise, not wanting to interrupt, and not knowing what else to do, Rod stood quietly until the man rose and extended a hand. While they shook hands, the man said, "Thanks, partner. I reckon you and the Almighty saved my ass this night. I done thanked Him. Now it's your turn. That was a close one, wasn't it?"

Taken aback by the simple, open display of faith from a man who had repeatedly shouted profanity in his ear, Rod felt the man's hand stiffen in surprise when he saw the white shirt. "Oh, God bless my Aunt Sadie. It's you, Mr. Silvana. Excuse me, sir. I didn't till this minute know I was talking to the big boss."

"Never mind. You have nothing to apologize about, nothing at all. Let's get you back to camp for another horse. I guess we still have work to do."

"Yes, sir. We still got much-a-plenty to do if we don't want to lose stock, but I think you got 'em turned good. Once they start turning into each other like that, they're likely to keep turning."

"I haven't learned everybody's name yet, I'm sorry to say. May I ask you to remind me of yours?"

"Well, there's quite a bunch of us to sort out, Mr. Silvana. My name's Buckner, but everybody calls me Sweetbean."

Rod laughed. "I remember you now. You're the one who brought your own jug of molasses for your beans, right?"

"That's me. Yes, sir."

"Well, if you're ready, let's mount up and go get fresh horses."

A moment later Rod asked, "Sweetbean, do you know which way to go?"

Buckner snickered. "It's right over yonder way, Mr. Silvana. Excuse me for laughing, sir, but we all took you for a lent. I'm here to tell you, lent or not, you'll do to ride the river with."

"Lent?"

"Greenhorn, sir, tenderfoot. We got all kind of names for people new to the cow business."

"Lent? Where did that name come from?"

"I don't know where words come from, sir. I just pick 'em up and use 'em whenever I find new ones. We say a man's lenty when his ignorance shows. Now I figure, when we get around this clump of trees and over that rise yonder, we might be close enough to see Cookie's light."

"Cookie?"

"The cook, sir. That ain't his name. That's just what everybody calls the cook. Sometimes sheffie, sometimes biscuit shooter."

"Right. I'll remember that."

Buckner cleared his throat, and Rod caught the hint. "Any more words I can pick up and use?"

"Well, that extra wagon that follows Cookie's, the men call it the hoodlum wagon, and the driver's called the hood. I heard you call it the baggage wagon the other day. That's what it is, rightly enough, but baggage wagon is lenty talk."

"Thanks."

"Yes, sir, you're welcome as rain."

When Rod saw the cook's light as Buckner had predicted and rode toward it, Buckner said, "Drop me off over yonder at the remuda. I got to get another horse and go back for my saddle. I think I lost a damn good horse this night. I'm just hoping the cattle didn't run over him."

"No help for it. No fault of yours, Sweetbean. I think this one could use some rest, too. He had a pretty good sprint before he had to carry double. Let's go by Cookie's wagon and see if he has anything to eat and some coffee. No telling when we'll have another chance."

"Uh, Mr. Silvana?"

"Yeah?"

"You might want to reload that pistol of yours, too. You know, it ain't worth much squeezed empty."

Rod reloaded without comment. Thinking back on his headlong rush to dress and get to his horse, he couldn't remember strapping on the Navy. He had watched with distaste when many of the men rolled into blankets after removing only hats, boots, and gunbelts. Reluctantly, he thought he might have to consider doing the same.

The idea of sleeping in sour, sweat-soaked clothing repelled him, but the possibility of being caught in front of more than three thousand panic-stricken cattle focused a man's mind on saving time. He realized Milt had given him a gentle hint about keeping a night horse saddled. Milt had also given him room to figure out the rest by himself.

At the first hint of light in the east, Rod rode from camp again with a sack of biscuits, each split to cover a slab of bacon, and spread them among the hands he could find. Most of the men would miss two meals and ride two horses ragged by the following afternoon.

Just before sundown the next day, Win rode out to join Rod on the western flank of the mile-long herd. "The count comes out good. I don't think we lost any cattle. All we lost was a whole day and a night's sleep."

"Lucky."

"Milt thinks we've got hair in our butter."

"I haven't seen him since the stampede. What's bothering him?"

"He thinks somebody is spooking the herd on purpose."

"Win, Milt was born suspicious."

"I know, but that isn't the sad part."

"What's the sad part?"

Win, fresh cigar in his mouth, paused to give Rod a long look. Then he struck a match with his thumbnail and cupped his hands around the flame. "He's damn near always right."

Win picked up a new wagon for the calves when they passed Gonzales, and the drovers immediately started calling it the blat wagon. Motherly instincts developed overnight. The drovers found it necessary to ride by at every opportunity to speak to the lovely driver and check her charges.

Milt, nodding in the direction of a couple of drovers riding beside the blat wagon, told Rod, "Never mind the calves. Those boys just want to make sure that sweet sorrel filly with the big blue eyes doesn't suffer from loneliness."

Rod got a snicker and a slap on the shoulder when he responded, "Profound observation. I'd never have guessed."

Most of the calves grew strong enough to keep up with the slow-moving herd after two or three days on the blat wagon. Milt traded the weaker ones for eggs and fresh vegetables whenever they passed close to a homestead with a big garden.

One day Rod asked Milt what the settlers did with such small calves.

"Some put them on a fresh cow. Some bottle-feed them till they get big enough to graze. Some feed them to the hogs."

"To the hogs?"

"Yeah."

"For heaven's sake." Back at Cowan's Fort, Cris had commented that Milt almost always answered questions truthfully but in the most shocking and nauseating manner imaginable. Her smile fooled him. Rod wrongly thought her warning a joke.

Milt showed his hard smile. "Lots of these folks let their hogs run wild, Rod. They have nothing to feed them most of the time, so they let them run free to live on what they can hustle for themselves. You've heard the expression 'root hog or die,' haven't you?"

"Yeah. Never thought much about it."

"Poor people don't waste things. You expect them to spend a day digging a deep hole to bury a calf? You expect them to get dressed up and have a graveside service? A sickly calf that isn't going to make it can still be good for something."

Rod rode deep in thought. Milt's comment triggered the sour realization that he faced a daunting challenge. The chasm between him and these men had never loomed so wide and deep. He spent far more for clothing each year than these fellow earned. In fact, he calculated that he spent more on casual gratuities to waiters and baggage handlers than these drovers earned. At twenty-five dollars a month, Nello Banks could only make three hundred dollars a year, if he could find regular work. Rod won or lost more than that with cool alertness, but without concern, on the turn of a card.

Given a chance for calm thinking, Rod found no oddity in the behavior of Nello Banks's sister. Facing such poverty, any reasonably intelligent woman would apply herself to menial tasks to save her brother a few dollars. She would consider the work so important that, in her ignorance of proper servant conduct and sense of dignity, she would grate on the nerves of a man accustomed to highly trained, discreet service.

Either she was easing the pressure a little each day or he was getting used to her. He no longer felt like a bug under a magnifying glass. He still drew discomfort from the thought of her poking around in his belongings, but she learned his habits quickly and stayed out of his way. He never rose too early to frustrate her obvious determination to have hot water ready and waiting for him to shave. A hot cup of coffee always sat steaming beside his shaving basin. At least, thank heaven, she had stopped watching him shave, standing nearby like a nervous mother waiting for him to slash a fatal gash in his face.

He couldn't fault her sense of discretion. He judged her conduct toward the men to be friendly with a deft touch of distance. The cowboys treated her with timid respect, probably because Nello became popular with all the men. Like his sister, he was eager to please and quick to learn. Win had him riding drag, the worst job of all, for it had him eating dust all day every day, but he never complained.

Milt broke the silence. "Sweetbean's been doing some talking."

"What about?"

"He's been telling about when his horse fell out from

under him. He rolled to his feet but says he thought he was finished. Out of nowhere, you came riding belly button to the sand." He paused to send a sardonic glance at Rod. "That's Texan for riding fast as hell."

At Rod's nod he went on, "He says he felt his horse going down and was able to land running. Then you snatched him off the ground like he was a stray pup. Says it felt like he'd been caught on an iron hook, thought he'd been gored. He's been showing off his bruises. Matter of fact, I saw that damage myself. You sure put your mark on that boy. Could count your fingers on his hide plain as day. I never saw the like, to tell the truth."

They rode without speaking for a hundred yards before Rod asked, "So what, Milt? I know you don't talk much when you're riding. That means this is important. I don't get it. What difference does it make?"

Milt finished his habitual scan of the surrounding country and looked straight at him. "It means your cards are faceup now, Rod. Sweetbean saw your hole card and told everybody. No use pretending to be a soft little rich boy any longer. He's telling the men you nearly broke his back, that his spine rattled from top to bottom like cracked knuckles when you grabbed him. He said you reloaded that Navy of yours wearing gloves, on horseback, in the dark, quicker than he can load his at high noon sitting in a chair. He's telling everybody the big boss is a bad man."

"He thinks I'm an outlaw? Why would he say that? I gave him no cause."

"A bad man in Texas isn't necessarily an outlaw, Rod, but he's damn sure a dangerous man if crossed. Some consider that a compliment in these parts."

After another silent ride, Milt asked, "You hear what I'm saying? Don't expect to surprise anybody."

"All right."

Milt turned his horse and cantered away.

EIGHT

"WE'LL BE COMING up on Waco soon," Win said.

Rod looked up from cleaning his Navy. "Seems like we've been driving cattle forever." The sun had nearly set, and the evening light put a soft glow across the rough camp.

"We've been lucky and unlucky so far. It's been a dry year, so the weather's been warm and sunny, and we haven't had to cross any swollen rivers yet. That's nice, but the trade-off is we have to choke on dust more than usual. I want to be one of the first herds to Abilene this year. Everybody made money last year and talked their heads off about it. This year everybody and his brother is trying to take a herd north. If we stay ahead of most of them, we'll get a better price."

"Good thinking."

"We'll have better grass, too. I'm taking us up the Chisholm trail, Rod. We took it last year and liked it better. The Shawnee trail isn't worth the trouble anymore."

"I'd never know the difference. I don't know where I am most of the time anyway. Trouble?"

"Too many farmers. They come out and try all kinds of crazy stunts, like trying to collect damages for crops they didn't even plant. They gang up and threaten to shoot both drovers and cattle. I've heard stories that some of the sheriffs even try to collect toll charges to cross their jurisdiction."

"That's your decision, Win. I trust your judgment. Is the Chisholm a longer route?" Rod reloaded his clean Navy and holstered it. He came to his feet and joined Win in an aimless walk. The restless redheaded trail boss talked more easily on the move. Win limited his conversation to a few terse comments unless he could move around, and Milt wouldn't eat in the light at night, always retreating into the darkness.

Rod smothered a smile, knowing both these strange men found him to be equally odd. They couldn't imagine exercising with weights on a trail drive, nor could they fathom his habit of handling cards at least an hour almost every day, even after eighteen or twenty hours in the saddle.

Win grinned as if he shared Rod's inner amusement. "The shortest route to Kansas is the one with the most grass and water and the least trouble."

"I hear that."

"There's a new bridge in Waco. They call it a suspension bridge. We can cross the Brazos over it, if you want. They charge about ten cents per head, or so I hear."

"You think it's worth three hundred and fifty dollars?"

"Not this time, Rod. Not unless we get a lot of rain all of a sudden. I recommend we cross about ten miles upstream from Waco. As long as the river's down, we shouldn't have any trouble. Even so, that bridge is a wonder. It's worth the ride to town just to look at it. I hear it's the biggest bridge of its kind in the country."

"All right. We'll drive the herd around Waco. We

might as well ride over and look at the bridge, though, since we're this close."

"I'd really rather swing a hundred miles around Waco, Rod. That's a pesthole, full of crooks, thieves, cheats, outlaws. It's the meanest town in Texas, worse than Fort Worth. We'll stock up heavy on everything in Fort Worth when we get there. We won't have another chance to buy much of anything between there and Abilene."

Rod permitted himself a wry smile. "Even if we ride around it, some of the boys won't like passing by a town without looking for a little fun. They need to buy things, maybe have a drink or two. Besides, it sounds like my kind of town. I've made a lot of money in places like that."

"We'll camp after we cross the Brazos and let them ride in a few at a time."

Rod nodded. "Whatever you think best."

"I put Miss Banks on the payroll. Seems to me you've decided to let her stick with us."

"List her by initials. Don't put anything in your expense book about her being a woman."

"Why not? If we hired a man to drive that wagon, we'd have to pay him. She's doing a good job—helps the cook, too."

"Win, my father has a sharp eye for anything unusual. I don't want to have to answer questions about her."

"Don't worry. I won't even have to change anything. I just listed her as A. Banks. I put her on at the same wage as her brother."

"A. Banks? You know, Win, she's been with us for three weeks now, and I don't know her first name. What's the *A* stand for?"

"Atha."

"How did you find that out?"

"I pulled a clever trick, Rod. I asked her."

"You're getting as sassy as Milt with your talk."

"I guess you've heard what they call Milt behind his back."

"They just call him Mr. Baynes around me."

"Well, when they aren't around you or him, they call Milt Comebacker."

"Curious name. How did that get started?"

"The Mexicans started it around Goliad when Milt mixed into trouble I was having. Being related to him, I guess you know he really isn't a normal person."

Rod's quick glance found no spark of humor in Win's expression. Win's steady gaze indicated that he caught the implied question, and he continued to speak with a no-nonsense tone.

"He doesn't have any quit in him. My enemies beat him nearly to death because he took up for me. When I say he took up for me, it sounds like I'm saying he patted me on the head and wiped my nose. It was a hell of a lot more than that. He drove off vigilantes and cut me loose from a hanging rope. Saved my life, that's what he did. Anyway, they jumped him a few days later and beat him to a bloody pulp, tied him on his saddle backwards, and sent him out of town at a gallop. He wandered all night, out of his head, I guess. I don't even like to think about the pain he must have gone through. An ordinary man would have died two or three times.

"His horse wandered back to my place the next morning. Milt was making strange noises like he was trying to sing. Scariest noise I ever heard in my life, gave me the chills. He recognized Cris, but he didn't even know me at first. Cris and I took him in and looked after him till he could move around a little bit on his own. As soon as he could sit a saddle, he rode off all alone to hide out. Cris thought he was going to leave the country. That was the only thing he could do that made sense, but I knew he planned otherwise."

Win paused, glanced around, and lowered his quiet tone another notch, the clear-cut actions of a man wary that he might be overheard.

"Sure enough, after he got about halfway well again, he came back and took on the whole town—the sheriff, the vigilantes, everybody. You never saw one man terrorize a whole chunk of Texas the way he did. No telling where he'd turn up next and then vanish again." Win paused and fixed cold gray eyes on Rod. "He never told you about any of this, did he?"

"No."

"Well, maybe it's none of my business, I guess, but it seems to me you ought to know."

"I was out of the country on business. My father told me Milt had a bad time, but he had handled it before my father could bring help. Milt never has mentioned it."

Win smiled and shook his head. "You ought to ask him about it sometime. Do it when I'm around. I'd like to hear how he tells the story. He broke me out of jail twice."

When Rod lifted a brow, Win said, "Yeah, I said twice. The first time, he and Cris threw black-powder bombs all over town. He caused so much damage the county judge called the army in to restore order, saying Goliad was in a state of civil insurrection. That didn't stop him either. He just kept coming back and raising hell, beating people up and shooting people and driving everybody crazy until either he killed them or they changed sides. He even ended up with Judge Bilbrey taking his side. They're great friends now. In fact, Milt and Cris got married in Judge Bilbrey's house. Cris sulks and gets snappish if Milt doesn't take her to visit with Susan Bilbrey fairly often."

"He'd probably twist the story all out of shape if I asked him, Win. He can't tell anything straight. I bet he'd just make a big joke out of it."

"No bet. That's what he'd do, all right. The Mexicans say he's the kind of man who goes and comes back whenever it pleases him, no matter what. I believe the Anglos think he came by the name from always having a quick comeback any time somebody tries to outtalk him. Milt's a sharp talker. He can cut down a blowhard fast as greased lightning. Either way, he's a comebacker. The name fits."

Their wandering brought them up to Rod's tent. "I think I'll get some sleep."

Win laughed. "It's not even dark yet. You're turning into a drover. Drovers sleep every chance they get. Good night, Rod."

When Rod flipped aside the tent flap and stepped inside, it took a moment for his eyes to adjust to the increased darkness. The warm, sweet aroma of cognac came strongly to him in the small enclosure. A white cloth covered his little folding table. The bottle stood in the center, flanked by two filled crystal shot glasses. He sank into his folding chair and lifted one of the glasses toward Lukie, who sat in the other chair. After the tiny clink when their glasses met, Rod took a tiny sip. "Drinking good cognac from a shot glass breaks my heart. You should have packed a couple of snifters. I'll never get used to hardship. What's the celebration?"

Lukie's answering chuckle hardly reached the level of a whisper. Rod had to lean forward to hear his next words. The unsurpassed eavesdropper, Lukie always lived in dread that someone would overhear his own conversation. "So you've decided we're going to tarry in Waco and make some money?"

"We might as well pick up some loose change if it's lying around. At least I can find my way around in a town. I prove every day that I'm not a drover. Why do you suppose my father sent me on this wild goose chase, Lukie? I'm about as useless on this drive as a fifth wheel on a wagon."

"You learning anything?"

"Yeah. The cook points the tongue of the cook wagon at night toward the north star so he knows the direction to start the next morning. Never try to drive cattle across a wide river against the sun. If they can't see the other side, they won't go. Homesteaders feed newborn calves to the hogs. I'm really learning a lot of useful information, very useful. When this is over, my conversation will make me the toast of Paris."

Lukie's hissing snicker barely broke the silence. "You got all these men on your side, Rod, all but two. Watch for one named Bright and another named Monk."

"What's wrong with them?"

"Troublemakers. I don't have anything against them yet but a feeling and little bits of talk."

"What talk?"

"The one called Bright, he said once that the big boss ought to pass the woman around a little among the common men. That fellow Sweetbean called him on it. Told Bright if he said that kind of thing again he'd kill him. Bright shut up and backed down real quick, but he's been sulking ever since. Sweetbean evidently has a tough rep, and I can see why. He has a hair-trigger temper, curses with every breath, prays before every meal, asks forgiveness for working on Sundays. Can't figure a man like that, deacon one minute and devil the next. I step light around all these Rebel white boys, but I'm most careful around him, and I'm not alone. Nobody gives him any back talk. Win Mill likes him, uses him for a straw boss when he needs one."

He stopped to sip his cognac, and Rod waited patiently. Lukie drank little and seldom but with such enormous enjoyment it gave pleasure to watch.

"What about the other one?"

"The one called Monk, he's been riding that kid Nello Banks. Nothing big, but just rides him all the time. Bright and Monk partner around. I got a bad feeling about those two, but I have nothing much but that, just a feeling."

The bottle seemed to float across the table to refill Rod's glass. Lukie's dark skin and clothing made him almost invisible in the gloom. "That's it for you. More than two when you're all tired out and you start to giggle." The slap of his hand seating the cork signaled his decision.

"Did you get ahead while you were waiting for me? Is that why you're so eager to set the cork?"

"Nope. Two for you this time and only one for me. That puts me one behind. You owe me one more out of this bottle."

"Win put the Banks woman on the payroll." Rod took a sip and waved the fragrant glass back and forth under his nose.

"Yeah, he asked me about it. I told him you'd hold still for it."

"The hell you did."

"Well, you did hold still for it, didn't you?"

"Yeah."

The cork squeaked, and the bottle floated over to fill Rod's glass again. "You get another half drink for being smart, just a little reward. Don't embarrass me. If you start to giggle, I'm leaving."

"You're leaving anyway. I'm sleepy. Go bother somebody else."

"Did you know that little Win Mill was a Union cavalry officer?"

"No. Nobody said anything about that. I'm finding out about everybody today."

"Interesting, isn't it, an ex–Union officer ramrodding a crew of Rebel drovers. Did you know he wouldn't hire a man unless he had both a rifle and a pistol and fifty rounds of ammunition for each?"

"The Banks kid didn't."

"No, but Mill made him promise to buy them when we pass by Waco. Mill paid wages in advance to some of our riders so they could buy what they needed."

"You been snooping around pretty fair. Where are you picking all this up?"

"None of this is a secret. These boys just close up around you. Nobody relaxes around the big boss. This fellow Mill talks to you and so does your cousin Milt, but they forget you don't know anything at all. It's hard to tell a person everything."

"Thanks. You always have something to say that makes me feel better. What's the reason for all the firepower?"

"Rustlers and Indians. You own about seven hundred stolen Mexican cattle yourself. Those men down on the border figured they were just stealing their own beef back. Ownership of some of these cattle isn't all that clear."

"Either Milt or Win told me about that, I forget which. That's no surprise." Rod grinned at the thought of someone glancing into his tent during this conversation. He and Lukie must be a sight, leaning across the small table, talking in whispers, faces almost touching over the bottle like a couple of tipsy lovers.

As if reading his mind, Lukie glanced at the closed tent flap before he spoke again. "Milt told me to expect most of the trouble from Waco on north into Kansas. He said since I work around the camp all the time, I should help watch the horses. Anybody who wants to steal our herd can do it easy if they can set us afoot. Milt says rustlers seldom try to steal a whole herd. They're usually satisfied with one or two hundred head, but they try to stampede the whole bunch to make the game easier for themselves. The Indians usually would rather steal horses, but they'll gladly take cattle if they're mad or hungry."

"So all of this we've been through up to now has been the easy part?"

Lukie's head bobbed in a tiny nod. "That's what Milt says. He says the real fun starts when we ride into thunderstorms and hail. Last year they lost a drover, the horse he was riding, and six head of cattle to one strike of lightning."

"Wonderful. I'm glad you told me that. I'll sleep better. Good night, Lukie."

"Milt said the man's rifle fired, all the cartridges in his pistol fired, and the man's belt buckle branded his stomach right through his charred shirt and pants. The iron shoes burned right off his horse's feet."

"I quit listening ten minutes ago, Lukie."

"Milt said for me to get under my wagon if big hail comes. The drovers strip off their saddles and sit down under them. They had four horses and twenty head of cattle killed by hail last year. They lost another thirty head when the herd stampeded."

"You're so full of good news I think I'll start calling you Sunshine. Good night, Lukie."

"He said all these drovers are real careful about how they wake up. They check before they move to see if a rattlesnake crawled in their blankets with them while they were asleep."

"You can go away now. Good night, Lukie."

"Do you think a snake would do that? He said they do it to get warm."

"I guess it could happen."

"Rod, if your father asks you to go on another trail drive, could you think of an honorable way to tell him no?"

"I don't think so."

"I could break both your legs. I'd wait on you hand and foot, and we could stay in New Orleans away from snakes, and lightning, and hail, and all of this gloomy stuff. You could play cards, and I could crack heads if any of those white boys tried to come at you from behind. We're good at that, Rod, you and me. We really are."

"Good night, Lukie."

Lukie paused. "I have a real suggestion."

"Let's hear it."

"Treat Miss Banks like a person. You don't even talk to her. Keeps her upset all the time. She's trying hard to please you, Rod. She can't figure you out. You're the kind and generous man who's letting her come along with her brother, even paying her for making herself useful, but you treat her like dirt. What do you have against her?"

"Good night, Lukie."

Rod could barely hear the sibilant breath of a snicker when Lukie came to his feet. "Good night, Rod."

NINE

A CRASH OF thunder snapped Rod up in such panic he found himself already on his feet when he awakened. He straightened from an instinctive crouch and grabbed for clothing. Charged air raised the hair on his arms and legs so that every move seemed to provoke a ghostly, light-fingered, probing caress. The thunderbolt that woke him, to be that loud, may have struck the camp. Another thunderclap slammed so close he lifted his hands and dropped into a defensive stance again, ears ringing.

Before he could pull on his boots a whirling wind gushed through the camp like a moving wall, and one corner of his tent sagged. He tensed for an instant, heart pounding with fear that he was caught in the path of a stampede, but he heard no clattering horns or blatting of terrified cattle. The wind must have pulled a tent stake loose, one of the stakes he had watched Lukie drive at least six inches deep in the hard earth.

He ducked again when water smashed down onto his tent as a solid mass. Instantly, the crushing rain con-

105

verted his tent from a comfortable, private place into a booming canvas drum. Through the fluttering tent flap, Rod saw lightning streak across churning clouds so constantly the night stayed bright with a flickering feral light. Yet, so much water filled the air he couldn't see the cook wagon only a hundred feet away.

Rain fell so hard and dense it drove his hat down to his ears when he stuck his head outside the shelter to look around. Rod's heart sank. Almost as soon as Win had chosen to ford the Brazos instead of crossing on a safe bridge, the heavens opened. His decision must have sent a signal felt in the sky.

In the ghastly skittering light, rivulets of water already half an inch deep ran and danced in a rolling boil. Then, in a brighter flash, Rod saw pea-sized hail bouncing a foot high. The roar of beaten canvas reminded Rod of the straining, tortured sails in an Atlantic storm, a gale he recalled had paled the faces of rugged sailors.

Someone shouted, "Hit the saddle. Try to hold 'em. If they run, head 'em north if you can."

Rod paced back and forth a moment, fists clenched. Again, he didn't know what to do with himself. Luck rode with him once, riding out at night like a damn fool. He didn't want to chance that again. Yet, it seemed he should do something. His head snapped up when the tent flap jerked aside and a shiny-wet, slicker-clad figure ducked inside.

"Evening, Cousin Rod."

"Hello, Milt."

"Heat lightning is about the prettiest thing can happen of a night. Too bad cattle are too dumb to enjoy it."

"I'm too dumb, too. I never saw anything like it. It's scaring me grass green."

"Scared me, too, when I first saw it. Nothing wrong with letting something new scare you. New things bring a thrill to the heart. Makes a man want to keep traveling. Never will forget the first time I looked a Comanche in the eye, him all dressed up and painted and waving his best knife. Now that's a real thrill."

"What happened?"

"My sweet little brother shot him. Ward was always quick, as you'll recall. But that Comanche dearly wanted to hug me tight, so he kept coming. Since Ward hadn't shot him good enough, I had to shoot him, too. Embarrassed Ward to death, bless his heart. Ward's always been proud of his shooting, and he deserves to be puffed up about it. That's sure enough the truth."

Tension drained from Rod's tight muscles so fast he wondered if it formed a pool around his feet. Milt's carefree nature could calm a madman's hysteria. "Are we just going to sit here and talk, Milt?"

"We aren't sitting yet, but that's a good idea. You know a better place to sit than right here?" Milt snared one of Rod's folding chairs, shrugged out of his slicker, and sank down with a comfortable sigh.

"What if the cattle run?"

"If they do, you got hired men to handle it. Of course, if they stampede this way, then we'll have to run out and jump on our saddles for a while. That brings me to a little hint I been meaning to give you. You need to take a piece of an old slicker or something and put it over your saddle on your night horse before you bed down. That's a good habit to get into. On a night like this, you can run out, jerk it off, and have a dry place to sit on. A wet ass can thusly be avoided, making it easier for a man to smile on a cold, rainy day."

"Seems like we ought to be doing something."

Milt lifted both hands palms up. "We are, Cousin Rod. We are, indeed, doing something. You're being the big boss, and I'm being the scout, the hunter for wild game, and the stray man."

"Stray man?"

"Yeah. When the cattle stampede and we lose some, I ride all around picking up strays and bringing them back. Sometimes local ranchers and other enterprising men hold the cattle for me. Sometimes they hold them so tight, I have to wave my pistol in their faces before they turn them loose. I don't have to do that much. Usually I just say my name and they shove those cattle at me. It pays to come from a famous family. We're both doing our jobs just fine, Cousin."

The corner of the tent straightened, and the sound of pounding came through the roar of rain. Milt stretched and said, "That Lukie was wound up in a ball under your wagon, eyes big as billiard balls. I suggested he might come fix your tent. He told me to go straight to hell, but I guess he had second thoughts about it."

Before Rod could answer, the world went quiet, as if a door had slammed on a noisy room. Surprised to be able to talk below a shout, he asked, "What happened?"

"It quit raining," Lukie said as he slipped inside the tent. He stood dripping wet, slicker folded into a thick pad on top of his head and cinched in place with his belt looped under his chin. Milt laughed so hard he nearly fell out of his chair.

Round-eyed, Lukie appealed to Rod while tugging at his belt. "What was I supposed to do? Rush out and get brained in a hailstorm?"

Milt stepped to the entrance and picked up a little round hailstone. "This isn't hail. This is big sleet." Before he finished speaking, the tiny ball of ice melted between his fingers.

Lukie slipped his folded slicker under his arm. "Looked bigger to me just a minute ago. Is that the way it rains around here? Like a bucket in the face?"

"Sometimes." Milt gathered his slicker and stepped outside. "Get ready to travel. If I guess right, Win will start moving right now, since everybody's in the saddle anyway. He'll want to make a run for the Brazos, just in case it starts to rise. Besides, he'll want the cattle tired and hungry when we get across. He won't let anybody go to town if the cattle are jumpy."

Milt had called it right. Rod figured the herd had

moved four or five miles by the time gloomy dawn light
filtered through black clouds. He rode a circle around the
herd and wore out a horse before noon carrying biscuits
and bacon to riders who had missed breakfast and had no
prospect for lunch. The lead steers crossed what looked
like ordinary ground except for scattered puddles. By the
time the cattle at the drag end of the herd arrived, they
struggled through mud churned more than a foot deep.

Win was sitting relaxed in the saddle on a low rise
when Rod found him. Accepting a bacon-filled biscuit
with a nod for thanks, he said, "We've got a trail-broken
herd now, Rod. They're rolling along just fine. We've
still got a few bunch-quitters to deal with that're more
trouble than they're worth, but I think we've shot most of
the worst ones, the skittish ones that always want to jump
and run."

When Rod nodded without answering, Win said, "We
ate the ones we shot, so they weren't wasted."

Again, Rod nodded.

"Funny thing. All the ones we had to shoot belonged
to you. All mine behave themselves." Failing to get a rise
out of Rod, Win shrugged. "Texas humor. That was
supposed to be funny. Actually, most of the beeves we
eat on the trail have strange brands or none at all.
Somebody else's beef always tastes better to a cattleman."

"You planning to cross the Brazos tomorrow?"

"I plan to cross this evening. By dark, we'll be on the
other side. Milt says we're only about five miles away
right now. He wore a horse to a frazzle getting there and
back this morning."

"River rising?"

"Some. Milt says if we want to cross easy we better
hustle, I want to get across quick, then I want it to rain
some more right away."

"Why?"

"Most of the outfits won't have money to cross the
bridge with their herds. The Brazos might hold them

back for a few days till it goes down again. That would give us a few days' more lead. That's where I want to stay. Caleb Cowan is ahead of us with Milt's herd and maybe a couple of other small outfits. I want to be among the first three or four to get to Abilene."

"Sounds like you're making a race out of it."

Win picked the last crumbs of his biscuit from his fingers, obviously in no hurry to answer. Finally he brushed his palms together. "You're the gambler, not me. I've had bad dreams about getting to Abilene and everybody saying they don't need any more beef. That'd mean we sit around waiting for a buyer to offer low prices while we pay drovers who eat like starved hogs."

"You think we might lose some cattle with this crossing?"

"Might. You got any more of those biscuits?"

Rod handed him the last one. He turned the flour sack inside out and flipped away the crumbs. "If we do lose some cattle, it'll be a shame. I figure they'll be yours, not mine."

Win winked to show he heard the jab. "I don't think we'll have bad trouble. Milt knows what he's doing, and he says to come on fast. The wagons are already a couple or three miles ahead. They'll be on the other side by the time we get to the river. If all goes well, the men can have a hot supper tonight. The herd should be as hungry and tired as the men, so they'll both be interested in filling empty bellies and getting some sleep."

Rod rode on the downstream side when the herd came to the Brazos. Win sat in the saddle on the far side like a human signpost, waving the drovers to point the herd right at him across the selected fording point. The drovers kept shouting "Close 'em up!" to each other. Gaps in the stream of cattle raised the risk that followers might have time to think it over and decide to stop or swerve away from the river. Mixed among the leaders, Sweetbean and another man swung ropes against the rumps of lead cattle trying to stop to drink. Then their

horses sank under them, and they slid from their saddles
to let their mounts pull them through the water. The big
white steer, the habitual front walker of the herd, struck
out for the far bank, only nose, eyes, and horns above the
current.

Rain started again and increased from a sprinkle, when
half the herd had crossed, into a downpour as the last
stragglers trotted onto the far bank. Milt rode up, water
streaming from his hat, and sang, "Rain, rain, come out
and play. Rain, rain, come block the way."

White teeth flashed in his dark face when his sardonic
grin widened. "Looks like Win called and heaven answered. Water rose a foot while we crossed, and it's still
coming up. Another couple of hours and we'd have had
hell."

Rod, without dismounting, pulled off a boot and
frowned at the stream of water he emptied from it. His
sock had migrated down into a roll around his instep.

Milt watched Rod struggle to jerk the sock back into
place with his one free hand. His head wagged sadly, and
his voice carried a load of false sympathy. "I tell you,
Cousin Rod. These sticky, loathsome trail drives make
things terribly difficult for a gentleman to maintain
immaculate grooming."

Rod emptied his other boot without answering. He
pulled up that sock and jerked the boot back on. Milt
turned with him to head toward the cook wagon. A
vagrant breeze blew across the tightly held herd right
into his face, and Rod closed his eyes with an expression
of disgust. "I can't get used to it, Milt. The smell of all
those cattle bunched together nearly knocks me out of
the saddle when the wind's just right."

Milt chuckled. "Doesn't bother me. It's just the smell
of money, Cousin Rod. That shouldn't trouble you."

Dusk in the rain thickened early into night, and the
camp huddled forlorn and miserable. The cook struggled
to keep his fire going on top of rocks he'd gathered

somewhere, partly protected from the drizzling rain by a makeshift canvas lean-to.

The Banks woman, dwarfed inside a man's slicker, met Rod in front of his tent. She shoved a tin cup of coffee into his hand. The fragrance halted his nod of thanks in midgesture and he froze with the cup half lifted.

"Lukie said you might appreciate a tot of brandy with your coffee."

"Miss Banks, a tot of brandy is usually just a small amount, perhaps a bit more or less than an ounce. This smells like brandy with a tot of coffee." He took a sip. His nose never lied. The mixture tasted like heaven.

"I thought, if a little made you comfortable, maybe a lot would make you cheerful. I've known you for weeks now, and I've never seen you smile. You never smile, do you?"

He smiled at her. "Of course I do. I smile every time a beautiful woman brings me hot brandy with a tot of coffee while I'm standing ankle deep in mud during a driving rain. . . . I think you'd never succeed as a barmaid, Miss Banks. There must be half a pint of spirits in this big cup."

"It's about half coffee. Lukie watched me pour it, but he just nodded like I'd done it properly. I'm sorry." She reached for the cup. "Here, I'll pour that out and do it right."

He grabbed her hand before he thought, and he pulled his cup away from her reach like a defensive child with a favorite toy. "No, no, no. Don't do that. I like it. It's perfect."

She stopped instantly and looked down at the captured hand. Rod released her as if he'd touched a hot coal, but his hand jerked back to hover protectively in front of his cup. "Beg pardon, ma'am, but you mustn't even think about pouring out twelve-year-old brandy. I doubt if there's any more of this quality to be found in the whole state of Texas. God would strike me with a bolt of lightning if I let you do such a thing." He exaggerated a shudder.

"Is it really that good?"

"Miss Banks, please have a brandy with me. I'd be honored."

"I'd better not, but could I have just a sip of yours?"

"Of course." He passed his cup to her.

Even in the increasing darkness, he noticed her hands, small but not delicate, with clean fingernails. Her eyes smiled at him over the rim of his cup when she tipped it to her lips, and he felt a powerful sense of intimacy. He had never shared anything with anyone but Lukie in this fashion, and he found it unexpectedly pleasant. Then her eyes went wide and she handed the cup back quickly. She pursed her lips, blew several times, and waved her hand like a fan in front of her mouth. Finally she said in a strained voice, "That's horrible. It burns."

He couldn't help smiling. "It's a strong drink to be taken carefully. One tastes brandy rather than drinking it. I should have warned you. I'm sorry."

Her straight gaze, once so disconcerting, no longer bothered him. "That's twice you've smiled in about two minutes. Brandy isn't good for me, but it does you a world of good."

"I drink seldom, Miss Banks, and then in small amounts. Strong spirits tend to relax people. That's not a good thing for a man like me." Rod scanned the quiet camp. Standing in plain view of anyone who might take interest while chatting in a heavy rain with the only woman for miles around made him feel foolish. He couldn't invite her into his tent. If he did, the camp would probably explode with talk. She seemed at ease and comfortable.

He found her smiling when his attention returned to her. "It's only rain, Mr. Silvana."

"Yes, it is. I guess I'm not an outdoor person, Miss Banks. All my life I've been taught to get under a roof when it rains. You and these men seem not to need a roof. You simply go on about your business."

"We do what we think is necessary, Mr. Silvana. Complaining about our work never makes it easier."

"I didn't mean to complain."

"No, you didn't. You never complain, but you never smile unless I remind you. Why?"

"I suppose I don't find much to smile about."

"Then you should look closer, pay more attention. We pass this way but once, Mr. Silvana. We should savor the one life we have."

TEN

THE NEXT MORNING dawned under low, dark clouds. The herd, allowed to spread after crossing the Brazos, grazed peacefully.

While Rod rode with him around the herd, Win said, "All the boys need to do today is keep them grazing in the right direction. We probably won't make five miles, but that doesn't matter. We just want to keep moving to fresh grass and keep the herd from scattering too much. Some of our men aren't interested, so we'll have a chance to let everybody go to town who wants to go."

Rod nodded and flipped an indifferent hand.

"I plan to stay with the herd, but I figure to let Miss Banks take the blat wagon in. She'd like to do some shopping, and she'll buy for the cook. Nello needs to buy some things, too." After riding for a while without comment, Win added, "It's not a bad idea to send a wagon in for those too drunk to ride back. I hate to tie a man in the saddle."

"I'll ride with the wagon," Rod said.

Win smiled and looked away. "I think everybody plans to ride with the wagon. The boys seem drawn to it for some reason."

"Good. If our men hang around Miss Banks, we won't have to worry about her."

"Matter of fact, Rod, I passed the word that at least two men must keep her in sight all the time. That doesn't count her brother. I'm giving the boys from nine this morning till midnight tonight. Three hours to get there and three hours to get back means they'll have nine hours in Waco to do their business, whatever that is."

"I doubt we'll have to worry about her, Win. Any woman who rides into town with ten men around her probably has no worries."

"I've come to think like your cousin, Rod. I don't like surprises, so I try not to let them happen. She won't be bothered if our boys make it real obvious they're watching her all the time." Win pointed to the blat wagon when the camp came into view. "Looks like they're ready to go. I guess they're just waiting for you."

"Where is Milt, by the way? I haven't seen him around."

"Milt has no use for towns, so don't bother inviting him to go with you. He's out somewhere watching and being sure he's not being watched. I guess I'm preaching to the choir telling you about Milt. You know how he is."

The slow ride into Waco became a joshing contest. Among other things, the men took a vote on who looked the most ragged. Nello Banks won by acclamation.

Waco, founded at the site of ancient Indian campgrounds on the banks of the Brazos, boasted a dirt main street recently converted by the rain from a dust strip to a mud track. With one swing of his eyes, Rod found the livery, four saloons, a blacksmith shop, two general stores, a hotel, a harness and boot shop, and one combination restaurant and bakery. He took a closer look before he found lettering painted on a glass window in a side door of the harness shop. Waco provided its marshal with a tiny office, but the town evidently didn't feel he rated space that opened on the main street.

Atha Banks pulled her wagon to a halt in front of the biggest general store, and the cluster of mounted men around her scattered.

Rod rode up beside her and said, "It's nearly noon. Let's go see if that restaurant serves good food."

She lifted her face slowly to look up at him and hesitated. Nello said softly from the seat beside her, "We got to save every penny, Mr. Silvana. We figured to skip lunch."

Rod put on what he hoped would be a charming smile. "I didn't make my invitation clear. I just offered to take the whole Banks family to lunch. Enjoy a treat on me. If the food's bad, we'll be sick together."

Her gaze dropped and she shook her head. "I really don't think we should—"

Rod interrupted her, and it made him feel good to give her a dose of her own medicine. "Good. That's settled. Just leave the team hitched right here, Nello." He turned his mount to cross the street without giving either of them time to respond.

After the meal, Nello and his sister picked their way back across the muddy road while Rod mounted and rode. When he dismounted, Nello said with a big grin, "You're sure enough becoming a Texan, Mr. Silvana, climbing aboard a horse to travel maybe twenty-five steps."

Rod winked at him. "Keeps my boots clean, too. Why don't you go ahead with your shopping, Miss Banks? I need a word with Nello."

She shot a curious glance at her brother before answering. "All right. I'll see you inside, Nello."

As soon as she stepped inside, Rod took a careful look around before he spoke. He stared into Nello's eyes, putting the icy expression on his face that he'd spent hours in front of a mirror perfecting. "Are you an honorable man, Mr. Banks?"

The boy flinched in surprise, drew himself up, and blurted, "I hope so, sir."

"Good." Rod, covering his action with his body so no one in the store could see, pressed five double eagles into the boy's hand. "Buy yourself a decent hat and some boots. Be generous with your sister. She needs lots of clothes and . . . and whatever it takes to make a lady comfortable. Tell no one, absolutely no one, about this. I want your solemn word on it."

When the boy glanced down and saw what lay in his hand, he protested, "Sir, Atha can't take such a gift from you. It wouldn't be fitting. Might start ugly rumors."

"Listen to me, young man. Your sister is receiving no gift from me. Do you understand? This is strictly between us men. Sometimes women don't understand such things, so it's better not to trouble them. No one must know about this but you and me. This didn't happen. If you say it happened, I shall be your enemy, and I shall call you a liar. If you should take offense at that and pull a gun, I shall kill you and suffer no remorse. If, for some reason, someone suspects and asks about it, sir, you will lie. I shall support you in that lie. Every gentleman knows that some lies are debts of honor."

Rod took another quick scan around before he said any more. He knew he was talking too much, but the young fool acted like he needed to be told how to wipe his nose. If word got out about this, no telling what kind of rumors might get started. It might even give her wrong ideas.

"As a man a bit older than you, I am merely advising you to be generous with your sister. If anyone hears of this, especially your sister, I shall know you to be a man of vile, wretched character whose word is worthless. That would sharply disappoint me. Now stand up like a man and give me your word."

The boy shifted awkwardly and gave a quick look over Rod's shoulder. "She'll know, sir. She's smart, and she knows how much money I have, down to the last penny.

Fact is, she looks after our money. She's older'n me, you know. She's my big sister."

Rod, stumped for a moment, removed his hat and smoothed his hair, trying to conceal his frustration. He tried to make the move casual, as if he and the young Banks discussed nothing of importance, as if they were having an idle chat. "Tell her Mr. Mill gave you an advance on your wages. Tell her anything but the truth. I'll get Mr. Mill to back you if she should ask him."

"What about when I get paid in Kansas? She'll expect my pay to be a hundred dollars short."

"Damn it, Nello. When you're paid in Kansas, put a hundred dollars in your pocket before she sees it. Have you no sense at all?"

"I can do that, sir." Nello smiled and nodded his head eagerly. "I can pull that off. But wait a minute. What if she asks why you cut me out of the herd for a private talk?"

"You have received a fatherly sermon about the evils of strong drink and loose women in this rough town. That's all." Rod tried to keep a cutting edge of sarcasm out of his voice. "Do you think you can remember all of that?"

"That's good. She'll believe that, I bet. That's real good, Mr. Silvana."

"Thank you. You must cultivate the ability to lie to women, Nello. If a man can't do that, he might as well be dead. Now go in there and buy your sister some nice things." Rod spun on his heel and walked toward the nearest saloon, feeling like a cad. The young fool's simple honesty shamed him. When Rod remembered Atha Banks's direct gaze, he grimaced and paused; he almost turned back, but the impulse came too late.

He'd look like an utter fool if he went back for his money. Yet, she'd probably see through Nello in an instant. The poor kid didn't have a chance against her, and that meant Rod had probably made an awkward mistake. He put it out of his mind and stood rubbing his

hands, idly loosening and warming his fingers while he
looked for a promising place to pick up a little money.

Promptly at nine that night, Rod walked out of the
saloon a hundred and thirty-two dollars richer, won from
hospitable citizens of Waco, since no other cattlemen
were in town. Lukie, sitting on a bench in front, rose to
join him.

Lukie said softly, "Went and got our horses an hour
ago. Wouldn't have surprised me if we'd had to leave
here fast. I got nervous when the town marshal invited
himself into the game. Lawmen are always crooked and
usually mean too."

Rod grinned. "He won a few dollars, so he was feeling
good about the game. He did it himself. I didn't even
have to help him." Two horses stood, heads drooping,
tied to the rear of the blat wagon. He raised his voice and
spoke to the group of horsemen clustered in the street.
"Everybody accounted for?"

A bleary voice came from one of the mounted men.
"All here, Mr. Shuffle, but two of our calves got colic so
bad they got to be burped on the blat wagon."

A burst of wild guffaws greeted the drunken sally like
the most sensational joke of the evening. Mirth tipped
the delicate scale in one man's head. He listed slowly to
the side, laughing fit to split, vomited like a tilted teapot,
and couldn't stop the lean. He fell into his own mess with
a boneless flop that splattered Rod's trousers. Lukie,
quick as a startled squirrel, leaped back in time to escape
the splash.

Ollie Broward, a sun-blackened cowhand from Brownsville, announced in a booming voice, "Lukie Freeman,
champion back-jumper, wins again on a muddy track.
Blind Shuffle froze in the starting gate and came in
plastered with mud." He took a deep drink from a bottle
and belched with such juicy gusto the man beside him
jerked away in alarm and then fingered his sleeve to see
if it was still dry.

Chuckling, the men loaded the fallen rider on the wagon, tied his horse behind with the two others, and snickered through a belching contest for two or three miles. Then Broward fell out of the saddle. He groped around in the grass on his hands and knees until Rod said, "Some of you men help him up."

"Don't need no help, Mr. Shuffle. I just need a minute to find my bottle."

"You dropped the empty a mile back. You men help him up."

But Broward insisted he could ride and fought off all offers of help. He got himself back in the saddle on the fourth try. When he fell a second time, Rod ordered him to climb on the wagon. Grumbling, he perched on the tailgate as if to prove he wasn't really too drunk to ride. When Atha started the team, he toppled off, not losing the posture of a seated man until he struck the ground.

"Keep going!" Rod shouted to Atha when she slowed the wagon. He rode back and leaned from his saddle to look down at Broward lying comfortably stretched out in the mud, smiling at the sky. "By God, Ollie, you can walk back to the herd if you don't get yourself up from there. Get on the wagon and behave."

"Walk?" The idea so shocked Broward that he sprang to his feet, only to lurch sideways for a few steps in a frantic, arm-wheeling dance to catch his balance. He straightened, looked up at Rod, and started to speak, but lifting his head tilted him over backwards. In the effort to catch his balance, he took a leap back and dropped to his haunches.

Rod heard the rip of the man's trousers clearly when his Spanish rowels drove deep into both buttocks. "Whoo ah-ah-ah!" Broward exploded from his crouch like a giant bullfrog, clutched at his spurred buttocks, and spun in a remarkably graceful pirouette before a boot slipped and his butt crashed into the wet ground again.

Atha stopped the wagon and called back, "That

sounded like someone screamed. What happened? Is someone hurt?"

Broward yelled, "I'm bit, Miss Banks. A rattler got me on my hiney-biney. I'm dying."

Rod called out, "Keep going, Miss Banks. He just sat on his own spurs." The wagon resumed its creaking forward progress.

On his feet again, the drover veered and staggered to catch up. He crashed into the tailgate and clung there, feet dragging, evidently confounded and trying to figure a way to climb aboard. Rod dismounted, grabbed the man's belt, and tossed him headfirst over the tailgate. Rod stepped back barely in time when Broward reversed himself like a startled crab to retch over the tailgate.

Rod shouted, "Keep moving, Miss Banks," and turned back to his horse.

Sweetbean Buckner sat in his saddle with a grin so wide Rod could see it in the dark. "Now that was a sight, boss. Don't know as I've ever seen a hundred-and-fifty-pound man pitched on a wagon so easy. It looked like nothin' at all, like tossing a feather pillow."

Rod swung up and asked, "Are we headed right to find the new camp? Mills said they'd move north."

"Think so, Mr. Silvana. They won't have moved much. I figure we'll catch the tracks and follow till we come up on 'em. No chance of missing the trail the way the cows chop up this soft ground. If we're too blind to see it in the dark, we'll smell it when we sink into it. We need to stop soon's we see Cookie's light, sir. We need to try to get those boys back on their horses. Mr. Mill won't be tickled, us coming back with half the men too unbuckled to stay in the saddle."

Sweetbean rode up beside the wagon, but Rod could still hear every word. "Nello, look back at those boys you got on that wagon every now and then. Don't let nobody lie on his back. We don't want nobody to drown in his own puke." He swept off his hat. "Excuse the blunt language, Miss Banks, but I don't know no other words for it."

He reined in until Rod came up beside him. "You done a smart thing, hiring that Miss Banks. I reckon that's why I'll never be a big owner. I never would have given that idea a second look. Me, now, I'd have figured having a woman along on a drive would be a headache. She's a fine lady, keeps herself busy making life better for everybody."

"Oh?"

"Sewed up one of my shirts I'd done give up on. Now it's like new. Saved me from having to spend a dollar to buy a new one. She even washed it before she gave it back. You see how she washes stuff for the men?"

"Haven't noticed."

"Smartest little trick I ever seen. She puts stuff in a barrel half full of soapy water she's got roped to the side of her wagon. The bumping and swaying of the wagon keeps the gear sloshing around in that barrel. By the end of the day, the stuff is plumb clean. She don't even need a washboard. Ain't that simple? Clever lady."

"Yeah, that is smart. Saves a lot of work."

"I wonder if a man could churn butter that way, Mr. Silvana."

"Why don't you rope a few fresh cows and ask her to give it a try? I guess she'd need another barrel."

They rode in silence awhile before Sweetbean said, "You ain't really pondering on having me do that, are you, Mr. Silvana?"

"No. I guess not."

He blew out a long breath. "Glad to hear that. You sure enough had me grinning like a possum eatin' yellow jackets. I got plenty enough to do without chasing mama longhorn cows and starting arguments."

Rod coughed to cover a laugh, but it didn't work.

"Well, I declare. You had me going, Mr. Silvana. Led me on like a newborn—and me sober, too, or close to it. I didn't figure you had no sense of humor at all, but I

should've known better. That cousin of yours, Milt
Baynes, now he's like me. He's got more wind than a bull
in green corn. You being so quiet, I didn't even suspect
nothing till you got me."

They rode in relaxed silence for about another hour
before Rod spoke again. "Do you see a light yonder,
Sweetbean?"

"Yes sir, now that you mention it. I'll go up and see if
I can tighten their hinges enough for those boys to stay in
a saddle. Mr. Mill ain't a hard man, but he don't use up
all his kindling to make a fire. He's all horns and rattles
when a rider gets too full of tarantula juice to work."

Rod maintained his plodding pace while Sweetbean
cantered forward to the wagon. Sweetbean Buckner rode
point, a prestigious position for a rider as he was
responsible for keeping the herd moving in the right
direction. Win Mill obviously thought highly of the man,
and the crew took his suggestions as if they were orders.
Buckner came from Brownsville, near the Mexican
border, so he probably spoke pretty good Spanish. Rod
wondered if he would understand the man any better if
he could get him to speak Spanish. It seemed to Rod that
he would be able to claim a fourth language if these men
continued to teach him to speak Texan.

ELEVEN

LANTERN LIGHT FLICKERED from the star on his vest when the marshal leaned forward to shove a folded piece of paper to Furnam. "The first name on the list is the buyer. The deal is, he'll pay five dollars less than the going price for beef. You sign a receipt for the going price. He stuffs five dollars per head in his pocket, puts the beef right on railcars headed back East, and nobody asks questions. Nobody gives a damn. He makes a big profit his backers don't know about. You make a big profit for rustled stock. Everybody wins. Nobody bothers to check brands on all those cattle going through Kansas."

Furnam unfolded the slip of paper and scanned the names. "I can find all these men except the buyer right here in Waco, right?"

Settling back in his chair in the saloon, the marshal nodded. "I've had a little rub, scrub, and rinse with every one of those boys. You're doing me a favor to take that trash out of my town. I'd be obliged if you'd bury them when you're through with them." He waited until Furnam looked up from studying the list before he added, "None of my business, but you boys aren't fixing to go after that Silvana herd, are you?"

Furnam said, "None of your business, but that's the one we want."

"Then you better look to your hole card. If it was me, I'd pick on somebody else."

Leach and Furnam sat across the table from the Waco marshal. Furnam, sweat beading his forehead, held up a bandaged left hand. "You ever have your hand stomped in a stinking boiler room? You ever get thrown overboard and have to swim for your life with three broken fingers and a broken wrist? I'll bet you never got taken for over a thousand dollars by a prissy little rich boy either."

The marshal shrugged. "It's your play. I've done my part. You got the names you asked for. You got a buyer who won't give you any trouble, and you got a list of riders I think will go for stealing cattle. You owe me a hundred dollars."

Leach slid five double eagles across the table under his hand, and the marshal swept them off the table and into his pocket without a glance at the coins.

Leach, his thin face haggard in the harsh light, asked, "You say you'd pick another herd. Why?"

"This is almost the first herd through this year, so everybody is excited about money coming into town. Everybody is curious and asking questions, and those hands talked real free. This herd's too big to swallow. They're moving more than three thousand head in that bunch. That outfit's traveling first-class, got plenty of horses, plenty of everything. They got over twenty drovers, and the word I get is that every man carries iron."

The marshal rubbed his badge and stared thoughtfully at the nearly full bottle on the table. After a five-second silence he reached a decision and poured himself a drink. After corking the bottle without inviting the others to join him, he lifted his drink to the light, saluted Leach and Furnam in turn and took a small sip. He spoke as if there had been no pause.

"You ever heard of the Baynes clan?"

Furnam and Leach shook their heads.

"I hear Milt Baynes is riding with this herd. I never met any of that Baynes crowd, but they got a bad rep. Milt treed the whole town of Goliad awhile back, and talk has it he did it all by his lonesome self. If half the stories going around about that Baynes tribe are true, a smart man might think long and careful before taking them on. Seems like they got lots of friends, and their enemies don't live long. Another thing—some Silvana riders come all the way from Mexican border towns. Those boys are always tough enough to swallow a horn toad backwards. Lots of herds come through here without such a big crew. Most drovers coming through here are kids never smelled gunpowder. This bunch even has a woman with them, a white woman. First time I ever heard of that. You hurt a white woman out on that prairie and the stink will reach clear to Chicago. Win Mill's the trail boss. He was a Yankee cavalry officer, and he don't leave no strings untied. I think you're barking at a knot."

Leach asked, "Barking at a knot?"

The marshal gave him a tired glance. "Wasting your time. Trying something dumb." He refilled his half-empty shot glass.

Furnam pointed at his bandaged hand. "I got a good reason."

The marshal leaned forward, elbows on the table, and shook his head. "Hell, man, shoot him in the back some dark night and walk away laughing. What's the matter with you? Business is business."

Leach gave the marshal a quick glance. "I think you're right. Broadman, the man working with Silvana on that boat where we found trouble, was tougher than I thought. He took a knife in the back, but he turned right around and killed my man. I think my man died without talking, and that was lucky for me. Broadman was only laid up a couple of days, but I figured that was good enough. Best for me to leave town and be satisfied."

"That was good enough for Broadman," Furnam said, "but that isn't near enough for this smug little dandy Silvana. I want to strip him down to nothing, make that puny little pink sissy suffer. I want to watch Silvana bleed to death one drop at a time."

The marshal settled back in his chair with a wry grin. "Don't try to bleed him at a poker table. He played with the best in Waco and walked out heavier than he came in. The plan was for me to sit in the game and throw him out if he hollered about getting skinned. That simple little plan has brought us more swag than you'd believe from these bragging cattlemen. We're still scratching our heads trying to figure out what went wrong. He seemed to smell every trap we laid."

He rubbed his chin and stared off into space for a moment. "It's irritating to get foxed by the likes of him, but I wouldn't go kicking at snakes by taking on a tough trail crew to get at him. Doesn't make any kind of sense to me."

Furnam said, "I want him and his money both."

The marshal raised both hands. "You do what you like. I'm paid off, and I'm out of it. Like I said before, if it was me, I'd give fifty dollars to a good back-shooter, have myself a drink somewhere lots of folks would see me while the job is being done, and then I'd forget it."

Leach said, "We'll think it over."

Furnam sent a poisonous glance at Leach, his mouth twisted as if he'd bitten a green persimmon.

The marshal emptied his glass, turned it upside down and perched it like a hat on the neck of the bottle. The bartender came from behind the bar and removed the bottle without a word.

"I'll mention one last thing, just because I'm feeling friendly. For this kind of job, I'd cast a net up in the Nations to get more help. You won't get far with the three

or four names you got from me. Lots of tough men up
there who'll do anything for a few dollars. Those boys
know that country. Those names I gave you, boys from
around Waco, they might not be interested in a gunpowder deal anyhow. Lots of difference between a thief and
a gunfighter. Besides, no need to steal cattle too soon and
then have to wear out three or four horses every day
herding them farther than what's necessary. I'd let them
get the herd close to Kansas before doing anything."

He pulled out a gold watch, wound it a few turns,
checked the time, and dropped it back into a vest pocket.
"I made about thirty dollars in that game today. I got a
feeling if I'd tried to make more I'd be regretting it right
now. That's life, gentlemen. A man shouldn't grab for
more than he's sure he can lift." He scraped back his
chair and rose. "Good night, men. I wish you luck." A
wave to the bartender and the lawman vanished through
the door.

Leach stared at the table through a long silence.
Furnam finally growled, "You still feeling chicken? You
about to whine some more? You look sick enough to
spew."

Leach slowly raised his head. "You have become
abusive lately, my friend. Would you like to take back
that chicken remark?"

"Ah, now don't get huffy. You got to admit you've
been dragging your heels."

"I'm out."

Furnam's eyes widened and his mouth went slack.
"Out? What kind of talk is that?"

Leach leaned forward and stared into Furnam's eyes.
"I think the marshal's right. This is insane. I'm a gambler
and a confidence man. Towns are my hunting ground.
Tricks are my style, not muscle and guns. I always work
alone or with one partner. Gangs make me nervous."

He settled back in the chair and smoothed his coat,
smiling as he caught Furnam's attention focused on the
hand that paused close to his derringer. "I guess I don't

trust crooks. They're all too much like me. Besides, a good take dwindles when it has to be split too many ways. You gather your gang and do this job on your own. You're the stagecoach robber, the rustler, the gun man. As my last wife used to say, you can't team a catamount with a coyote, so we don't make good partners. I'm not even comfortable on a horse.

"That young Silvana you hate so much showed me I'm not even a first-rate card cheat. He rattled me like a dry gourd. You do him an injustice. He didn't give a fig what happened to us. He had nothing to do with it. The captain of that boat and Broadman could have fed us a champagne supper for all he cared. What I wouldn't give to have him for a partner . . . cold as ice, no sweating, no cursing, no confusion. That boy never got his hands dirty in his life, and he acted like he'd just as soon kill you as buy you a drink. I'm going back to Indianola and catch a boat for Cuba."

The smiling little confidence man's next words came out dripping with open contempt. "If you want to ride around shooting at people and chasing smelly cattle, that's your game, not mine. I hire thugs for work like that, and they always come cheap."

Furnam glowered through thick brows and wiped the back of a thick hand across his forehead. "You just took a lot of words to say you're yellow."

Leach rose, smile still fixed on his face. "Yes, I did, didn't I? Well, I know my limits. I could kill you right now, swine face." He leaned forward deliberately and slapped Furnam. When the big man didn't move, Leach's smile widened. "Why don't you reach for a gun, pork gut?"

Furnam's face whitened, but he sat perfectly still, hands flat on the table.

"I think you just found your own level of courage—and not a second too soon. As these savage Texans would say, you're all gurgle and no guts."

He backed out of the saloon without taking his eyes off

Furnam, smiling all the way, and left the swinging doors to creak back and forth behind him.

Furnam pulled out a soiled handkerchief and wiped his neck around a stained collar grown too tight. He'd almost talked himself into his grave. That dried-up little weasel couldn't hit a train station beyond about twenty feet, but at arm's length he couldn't miss, and he was spooky fast in getting that little parlor gun of his into play.

Good thing for him he'd seen the little fiend practice. He wouldn't have believed it if he hadn't seen it. The scrawny little bastard could pull that gun like a magician, and he'd had a killer's shine in his eyes for a minute there. Furnam licked his lips and realized his mouth had gone so dry he couldn't have spit for a hundred dollars.

The Waco marshal gave good advice, and it fit in this case. Fifty dollars to a good back-shooter wasn't all that much money, but downing a nervous little card cheat shouldn't even cost that much. After all, Leach ought to appreciate the irony. He'd said he hired out this kind of work, and he'd sneered when he said he got it done cheap. Furnam glanced again at the paper, now damp from his sweaty hand. It shouldn't even take long to find the right man.

He rose and sauntered to the bar. "Buy you a drink?"

The bartender put two glasses on the bar and filled them. "Obliged."

"I got some boys I'd like to find." Furnam laid a half eagle on the bar, keeping one finger on it.

"Waco ain't a big town, mister, and any friend of the marshal is a friend of mine. Who you looking for?"

Furnam slid the coin across the bar and pulled his hand away. "I always liked small towns."

Bright unbuckled the cinch and pulled his saddle off a tired horse. He took a careful look around the dark camp before he whispered, "Maybe another month and we start looking for the signal fires."

Monk, only an arm's length away, dropped his saddle to the ground and answered, "You talk too much. Are you too thick to learn? Your mouth almost got you shot once already. That Buckner can pull iron quicker'n you can spit and holler howdy. That feller's about as steady as quicksand. I ain't sure he's right in the head. He can't make up his mind from one minute to the next whether to curse or preach."

"Forget Buckner. I'm just looking to cross the Red. Hiram Redbone said that was the time to start watching. I'm tired of waiting, and I'm sick of being broke. Mill moves this herd so slow they're getting fat." Bright dropped his saddle beside Monk's and pulled off his gloves.

"I heard what Redbone said. I was there. Shut up about it, will you? Somebody hears you and we got bad trouble. That Milt Baynes sneaks around worse'n a Comanche. A man never knows when he's going to pop up out of the grass like a sage hen. He's another one gives me the creeps. He ain't normal. I still can't figure out when or where he sleeps. And you keep wanting to babble. You afraid you'll forget what to do if you don't talk about it every day?"

"I ain't scared like you, Monk."

"You ain't smart like me, that's the difference. I didn't have to buckle under and back up suckin' wind like you did. Buckner's just waiting for you to say one more word about that woman. You know that?"

"He don't scare me. I'm just saving him for later. Soon's we cross the Red and bust up this herd, I'll settle with him."

"If a man like Buckner don't scare you, you got less sense than a headless chicken. We got jobs to do. You stirred up hard feelings over nothing just by letting your mouth keep running after your brain went to sleep. Hard feelings don't put money in your pocket. You ever think about that?"

"I got along before I met you, Monk. I can get along without you again."

"I'll give you a break, Bright. I been living good on the owlhoot trail for more'n ten years now, so I've learned a thing or two. Ain't nothing to stealing cattle. Ain't nothing to stealing horses. Stealing is easy. Getting away with it is always the hard part. You think on that."

"Thanks. I'll be up the rest of the night trying to sort out all that thinking I got to do." Bright raised both hands to his head. "I ain't sure my poor bean can swell up enough to hold it all."

Monk stared with such quiet menace Bright dropped his hands and rubbed abruptly sweaty palms on his shirt. Monk leaned closer and spoke right into Bright's face. "More times than not, I got away because I didn't leave nobody behind mad enough to come after me with blood in his eyes. Remember, Bright, every enemy you make, every man you shoot, every one of them has friends and kinfolk. Enemies don't hide you out or hold fresh horses for you. I ain't never had to pick lead out of my back nor spend time in nobody's jail."

Bright snickered and eased a small step back. Something about the smaller man's fixed stare made his stomach tighten. "Me neither. I ain't no jailbird."

"You'd have trouble staying alive in a jail. You cause trouble before the right time and you'll face Hiram for it. If he takes offense, he'll wring your neck. I never heard of anybody surviving one of Hiram's tantrums. Ponder on that and see if you sleep easy. I'll take these horses over to the nighthawk. Drag my saddle over yonder by the fire."

Monk grabbed the reins of both horses and straightened, "Drop my saddle and walk twenty steps before you drop yours. I don't want to talk to you no more. You hear? Not another word until we cross the Red and see Hiram's fire."

Bright watched the shadowy outline of Monk and the

two horses fade into the darkness. He scratched an armpit and considered leaving Monk's saddle where it was, just to show the stumpy little cow chip he wasn't anybody's boss. On the other hand, Hiram Redbone's tone of voice when he spoke to Monk showed consideration. He bluntly told other men what to do, but he asked Monk. Monk always did what was asked, but the difference weighed heavy. That alone gave warning to a smart man that lumpy little Monk was worth watching.

Hiram Redbone's face still made Bright shrink a little every time the memory of it came to him. A ropy white scar trailed from under a patch covering his left eye across a nearly black cheek to disappear in the hair behind his ear. The knife that caused that savage wound had evidently removed the lower part of the man's left ear. His right eye was such a washed-out color it reflected firelight like a cloudy glass ball with a candle behind it.

Monk said Redbone probably wasn't Hiram's real name. Nobody knew, nobody cared, and only a damn fool would even think of asking his real name. Monk said Louisiana redbones were people of mixed Negro, Indian, and French blood. Some Louisiana folks took offense if a man called them a redbone. Hiram's taking that name had meaning. A man who picked a name that invited insult showed a wicked confidence, his attitude an open challenge to the world. Until he met Hiram, Bright had never seen a man carry two pistols at the waist and two more on his saddle.

Bright picked up both saddles and walked toward the camp. He dropped Monk's near the fire where he couldn't fail to see it. Then he counted twenty steps before he dropped his own. He flipped out his tarp and unrolled his blankets.

The ride to the Red River shaped up to be a lonely trip. Since he had tried to make a little joke about the boss's woman, the whole crew had gone snippy as a cluster of choirboys. Now even Monk refused to pass the time of day. One dark night, when Redbone hit this bunch, the youngest of the Bright boys would be ready to enjoy shooting at a covey of choirboys. It wouldn't be cause for grief if Monk happened to get in the way. Yeah, looking forward to that frolic put a better taste in a man's mouth.

TWELVE

"LYING IS SO complicated, don't you think, Mr. Silvana?"

Rod gave Atha a fake look of mild surprise. "Lying?" He forced a relaxed manner, knowing he'd just heard a verbal warning shot. This didn't sound good at all.

"Yes, lying." Atha straightened from arranging his plate in front of him. The lowering western sun softened the outline of the chuck wagon behind her and sent a long shadow across the trampled grass. She stepped back and smiled, but not before he caught a fleeting hint of the perfume she must have picked up in Waco. Smelled fresh, like expensive soap. Maybe that's all it was. She wore a new dress, nothing fancy, buttoned up all the way to her chin, gray and plain, a practical, durable garment. At least she didn't look threadbare and sun bleached anymore.

"What put you to thinking about something like that, Miss Banks?" He'd pretend innocent curiosity. No other choice seemed to make sense.

"Your attempt to get Nello to lie to me in Waco last week. What else?"

"Surely you're joking. Why would I do that?" He picked up a fork and focused his attention on his food. That damned Nello. No wonder he'd been ducking around. The kid jumped on his horse and faded away every time Rod came near him the last few days. He must have got his story tangled, made her suspicious.

"I've been wondering the same thing. Why would you do that?" She studied him openly, smiling like he were an amusing curiosity, a hairy bird with one wing and two tails. When he didn't reply, she seated herself on one of his folding chairs and added, "Seems to me you'd do it yourself."

"Do what myself, Miss Banks? I'm having trouble following the conversation."

"Do your own lying, Mr. Silvana."

No doubt left. She planned to pick a fight. She'd put on a new dress, perfume, and a sweet smile as a man would've buckled on his sword and hoisted his shield. No telling what Nello had told her. She might be thinking mighty near anything.

"You must take care, Miss Banks. I think you come near insult. Calling a man a liar is not a joking matter."

"True. I understand that, but I don't know what to call a man who gets someone else to lie for him. Is there a name for that?"

He put down his fork. She sat with her back to the light, her face hidden in shadow and the setting sun perched exactly on top of her head, perfectly positioned to dazzle him and hide her expression. He knew she had picked her spot on purpose; he saw the signs of a planned ambush, carefully timed. He sat still, feeling trapped, wishing for an escape route, hoping for an interruption. Maybe it would rain. He flicked a glance at the cloudless sky.

"Well?"

"Well what, Miss Banks?" He tried another look at her.

"What do you call a man who gets someone else to do his lying for him?"

He shrugged and lowered his head, blinking away spots that danced across his eyes. Damned if he'd look her way again. "Clever, I guess."

The sound of her pulling her chair closer tempted him for a second, but he fought off the impulse to risk another glance at her. He'd have to squinch his eyes against the sun and end up with his face twisted like an idiot with his finger caught in a coffee grinder. Either that or he'd be stumbling around seeing bright specks the rest of the evening.

"I considered that," she said softly, her tone low enough to ensure privacy. "Clever didn't seem to fit. Maybe timid. Perhaps shy? I even considered sly. The right word doesn't seem to come to me. None of those words fits you."

"Miss Banks, you have the better of me. Just what lies am I accused of tempting your brother to tell?" Might as well find out how much damage that fool Nello had caused. Not knowing built a wall of disadvantage, and she'd nail him to it if he didn't play a cautious game.

"You got him to say that the money you gave him came from Mr. Mill instead of you. You told him to say that the money was an advance on his wages. It seemed odd to me, since I had asked Mr. Mill for an advance on both Nello's wages and my own before we left for town. He gave me a hundred dollars, Mr. Silvana. He said he wanted me to have enough for Nello to have a new hat and new boots and spare shirts and trousers. He also wanted me to have what I might need on a long trail."

"Miss Banks, you mistake poor coordination for lying. Mr. Mill and I must have simply had the same idea but failed to discuss it with each other."

"What idea, Mr. Silvana?"

"That you might need some funds right now, rather than having to wait till we get to the end of the trail."

"Yes, that occurred to me, but then why would Mr.

Mill ask me not to mention anything about it to you? He said you weren't to be bothered, and such things were his job to look after anyway, but you were a stickler for modesty and decorum, and I should absolutely have the necessary clothing and 'appropriate female comforts.'"

"That's right. Quite correct. Everything in good order. Mr. Mill knows his job very well, Miss Banks."

"Yes, he seems very competent, and talking about him is an interesting diversion. But we were talking about you and my brother."

"Your brother seems nervous and ill at ease around me lately. Maybe he fell into a little confusion during our brief conversation."

"Yes, he's upset. He told me you threatened to shoot him. If you were joking, why isn't he laughing?"

It couldn't be worse. Atha had turned the kid inside out. He must have recited Rod's comments like a memorized Sunday school lesson to his sister.

"Possibly a poor joke of mine, a careless manner of speech. I'm not a threat to Nello, Miss Banks. I apologize if there has been a misunderstanding." Rod smiled in her general direction, thinking: *I'm no threat to that little coyote—beyond twisting his neck. Your brother will only see backwards the rest of his life after I catch him.*

"You think you need to be hard and tough, don't you? You don't want to be caught in an act of kindness."

Rod didn't know where that comment came from, and it caught him unprepared. He made no attempt to cover a puzzled expression. "You still have the best of it, Miss Banks. You accuse me of ordering your brother to lie to you. You think I threatened to shoot him. And you believe I'm guilty of concealing kindness. I'm afraid I'm too tired to follow your thinking."

She came to her feet, casting a shadow across him at last, extended a hand, and soundlessly slipped a stack of five double eagles to stand beside his plate. "Nello and I are grateful, and we both thank you for being so thoughtful, but it's too generous a gift. It wouldn't be proper for us to accept it, especially since you made it clear you expected him to buy things for me."

Rod cleared his throat, staring at the neat little stack of coins. The worst had happened. Now she thought he had made a crude attempt to buy her favors. Rod felt his face heat. "I just wanted to—"

"I know. You just wanted to avoid appearing to make an improper advance."

She had done it again. She had interrupted before he could get the words out of his mouth. She had stopped doing that lately, and he'd forgotten how it irritated him. If he wanted to say anything to her, he'd have to throw words like a person pitching water from a bucket, all in one abrupt stream.

Rod cleared his throat. "I was about to say . . ." Now he changed his mind and stopped in the middle like a simpleton. Anything he said now would probably make the situation worse.

But she stepped in so quickly it didn't matter. "Don't be so gloomy, Mr. Silvana."

He looked up at her. "I'm not gloomy."

"Certainly you are. You think a man might as well be dead if he can't lie to women, and you can't do it well, so you pushed Nello to do it for you. That's awfully gloomy. You might find happiness in spite of such a terrible handicap. I've heard of stranger things." She walked away, leaving him rubbing his mouth and hoping embarrassment didn't run off him and form a puddle around his chair.

He looked around to see if anyone saw his humiliation. She'd nailed down every corner of his hide. He'd have to avoid Nello for a couple of days, give himself time to cool. Otherwise, he'd beat that kid to death with a thorny mesquite stick. No, it wasn't the kid's fault. That's what really made Rod sore. The mistake was his alone. He should have known better.

He should have told Nello, "Take this money and keep your mouth shut." Then he should have walked away, walked away real fast. He should never have mentioned Atha at all. No, it would have been even better to let Win handle it. He should have kept his distance.

As if the thought called the man, Win came into sight. He rode into camp, dismounted, and walked up to Rod's little folding table. He glanced at Rod's plate and lifted a brow. "You're not hungry?"

"Let me see the expense ledger."

Win straightened, eyes suddenly wide, and pulled the tally book from inside his coat. He dropped it on the table. "Got a problem? You sound like you're sitting on a boil."

Rod turned pages until he found the last entry and started checking back from there. "I don't see it, and I'm already back to entries dated two weeks ago."

"See what?"

"Where you gave an advance to those Banks people."

Win rubbed his hands together for a moment and shrugged. "I didn't put it down. Just gave the kid a few bucks. I took care of that myself. Didn't amount to anything."

"Gave it to the kid, you say? Out of your own pocket?"

"Well, I gave it to the sister, actually. Won't put me in the poor house."

"A hundred dollars?"

"Who told you that?"

"Atha."

"Uh-oh." Win lifted both hands, rolled his eyes skyward, and made a sour mouth. "I told her not to bother you."

"You redheaded son of a bitch."

"No need for you to get huffy. Nothing to do with you." Then he focused on the stack of coins beside Rod's plate. "What the hell is that?"

"That's my hundred dollars Atha just threw back in my face because my own trail boss poisoned the well for me. Now she thinks I'm a lying, sneaky, clumsy fool."

"Why?"

"I slipped the money to Nello and told him to tell her it was an advance on his wages from you. He didn't think he could get away with it, so I told him a man might as well be dead if he couldn't lie to women, and I'd shoot him if he told her it was money from me. Nello went and told her every damn word I said. She cracked him like an egg, I guess, and ate him alive, guts, feathers, and all, since she'd already got money from you herself. Of course, you didn't say a word to me about giving her anything, so I fell in a deep manure pit and pulled Nello in with me."

Win shook his head and flipped a hand like a man bothered by gnats. "Oh, well, no real harm done. She'd find out you're a lying, sneaky, clumsy fool sooner or later anyway."

Rod swept the coins off the table and held them out in a fist toward Win. "Take this money."

"Why?"

"You didn't bring them along to raise. They're my blunder."

"No you don't. You don't get away with that. We're both guilty. No, that's not right either. It was my mistake. You were caught by surprise until it was too late to back off."

"That's the truth, but I had time to do something sensible later. I just didn't have the guts." Rod slapped the double eagles back on the table. "We'll flip. The loser has to take the hundred back. At least you kept it off the expense books. I'll give you that." He pulled a coin from his pocket and spun it into the air. "Call it."

Win said, "Tails."

Rod snatched the coin out of the air and displayed it with a theatrical flourish. "Heads. Take the hundred."

Win grabbed Rod's wrist before he could pocket the coin. "Let me see that." Rod didn't resist when Win plucked the coin from his hand. Win turned it back and forth and then returned it with a sheepish grin. "I thought you might have pulled a trick coin on me. I don't trust you."

"Satisfied?"

"Yeah."

"Good. You grabbed the wrong hand. The trick coins were in this hand." He showed Win the coins in his other hand, one two-headed and the other two-tailed.

Win laughed. "I ought to pop you one. I never saw but one coin and you had three palmed all the time. How do you do that? Did you pull a switch right in front of me?"

"Go get some sleep, sucker. And quit tampering with my employees."

Win picked up the money and shook the hand holding the double eagles suggestively, head tilted toward the musical clinking. "You know, we could go fifty each. That wouldn't be a bad thing. That way we'd be equally dumb and clumsy. Nobody would have an advantage."

Rod said, "I'm the boss. You got no business being as dumb as I am. I'm supposed to have the advantage. Besides, we already agreed to let the coin toss decide who keeps his hundred."

Win continued to shake the coins. "Nope. You're the big owner. I'm the big boss. We agreed, remember?"

Rod nodded. "You're right, but you're only supposed to decide about cattle. This is a personal contest to determine who's the most dim-witted. You want another chance? Tell you what, let's cut for high card. Whoever draws the high card decides what we do. I'll get out a fresh deck."

Win waved off the idea. "Hell with that. You'd cheat just to make me keep the money. I give up. No contest. I freely admit you're dumber than I am. I'm going over yonder to fall down and hope I hit somewhere close to my blankets."

He took a couple of steps away, turned around, and came right back. Standing close to Rod, he asked in a low tone, "You're taking a liking to her, aren't you? That's a fine-looking lady, mannerly and smart. Nice little package. I'd try to unwrap that, too, if I was still single."

"Don't talk foolish. She's too big for a shrimp like you. She'd throw you out with the bathwater and never know the difference. As for me, I can't even say good morning to that woman without her cutting in with some kind of chatter between good and morning. She hates to let me finish anything."

"Ah!" Win pointed an index finger like a pistol at Rod and leaned forward. "That's a sure sign. No chance for a mistake. She's taken a serious interest. You know a woman's getting attached when she takes over the talking for you. Pretty soon you won't need to say anything at all."

"Nonsense. She started interrupting me the day we met."

"Is that so? Decided quick, didn't she? My wife did that, too." Win strolled away into the dusk, still rattling the coins.

THIRTEEN

THE LAST STEAMING cattle slogged up the muddy slope and trotted to join the ones ahead, shaking water from waterlogged ears, and surging into brief sprints to escape ropes swung by soaked, hoarse drovers.

Win turned in the saddle and spoke in a relieved tone. "The Trinity is behind us now. Every river we cross gives me a nervous fit."

Rod nodded. "Cowan told me not to get in a snit when we lose a few head crossing water. You're too hard on yourself. We haven't lost any yet."

"Losing a few cattle I can take. It's drovers I'm afraid I'll lose. You know half our men can't swim?"

"Yeah." Rod pulled out a white silk handkerchief, doffed his hat, and wiped his face and neck. "I see them watching each other all the time, working in pairs."

"Right. Maybe we talked about this before. Sometimes I forget what ground we've covered. Anyway, I put a swimmer working with a nonswimmer. I also keep a good man with a rope on both sides of the river."

"Another thing for me to remember and hope I'll never use after this drive."

"Oh?"

"You act like this is just an ordinary job, nothing to complain about. It's the worst kind of work I ever saw. I'd rather be a stevedore at the New Orleans docks. At least I'd be able to get a decent night's sleep and breathe some clean air once in a while. This is one hell of a way to make a living. The only thing worse than this would be picking cotton."

Win slapped at swarming flies with his hat. "Wouldn't know. Never picked cotton."

"Me neither."

Win's voice came flat. "I'm going to fire Bright tonight. Thought I ought to tell you."

"Wondered how much longer you'd put up with him."

"You agree to it, then?"

"Don't need to. You're the trail boss."

"He's a complainer, Rod. Poisons the air. Ducks work and moves slow. Man like that can spread bad feelings, cause morale problems to get started among the other men."

Rod laughed. "Morale problems. I like that. Sounds like army talk."

"It is. It's straight talk, though. If I was still in the army, I'd have had him in the guardhouse about six times already for either malingering or disrespect. Sweetbean Buckner's one of the best men we have, and I use him as a kind of second-in-command, but he's notional and short tempered. Sweetbean spoke to me earlier today, said I got three choices. I can fire Buckner, fire Bright, or I can let Buckner whip Bright. Not much choice, really. If I let him whip Bright, at best the man wouldn't be any good for a week or two or, at worst, he might be dead. Buckner is very thorough."

"Why'd you pick tonight? Any special reason? You're moving fast."

"Main reason is I don't like him." Win flashed a hard

smile. "I'm not about to give him a horse, so I'm putting him afoot. Doing him a favor, really. He'll only have to walk a half dozen miles to Fort Worth. I figure to let him trip on his own loop. He'll surely put up a growl when I tell the men nobody can go in to town. That will give me an excuse to make an example of him. I'll just tell him to walk right on into town. While he's doing that, we'll be riding on all night."

Rod groaned. "Another night sleeping in the saddle. That's a thrill to hear. Makes me want to quit, too. Why's that necessary?"

"There must not be a dozen honest people in Fort Worth. Nothing there but card sharps, whores, and thieves. Every time a herd stops near that town, some-body tries to make the cattle run so they can try to steal a few. Last time I came through here I nearly shot a couple of twelve-year-old boys in the dark. They didn't even have horses. Little fools tried to run off six or eight head by waving sticks at them."

Win spat to the side. "Even their children try to steal. Trashy parents, trashy kids. Scares me to death. Maybe you'd like to think what might happen to a couple of little boys waving sticks at some of our longhorns at night. Would you like to try that?"

"Kid stuff, but that's another thing I don't want to do. I don't want to be a cattleman, I don't want to pick cotton, and I don't want to be a bullfighter. I have to say, though, bullfighters wear pretty suits and do right well with the women. Do we have all the provisions we need?"

"No. I'll be sending a wagon to get some more bacon and flour. I need to get another jug of molasses for Buckner's beans, but nobody gets time off for drinking or whoring."

"Fort Worth sounds like my kind of town, Win."

The remark brought another tight grin. "Owners do what they please. The boys know that. Won't cause a problem with the men if you go in and get your pocket picked or your head busted. They'll get a good laugh."

"Win."

Mill turned a questioning glance toward Rod at the tone.

"You fire Bright, but I'll give him his wages. Lukie says Bright made a comment or two about Miss Banks."

"Sounds like you got hard feelings. You planning something?"

"Yeah. Didn't want to make a move before. Didn't want to interfere with you running the crew. Now that you're firing him, though, I don't have to worry about that."

"Think it's worth the trouble? Bright's strong as a bull."

"Yeah. You say you need an example. Let's make a good one."

"Your call. I'll watch that fellow Monk. They hired on together, but Monk seems to be keeping his distance lately. Anyhow, we might have to deal with both of them."

"Lukie will tend to Monk if need be."

"You might not have time to tell Lukie. I figured to fire Bright before supper. I'm a mean man. I plan to send him off hungry."

"If you fire him before supper, I'll be ready. After that he won't be hungry."

"You sound mighty sure."

"Bright made the mistake of talking down to Lukie. We've been together all our lives. Lukie and I, we plan ahead. He looks after me, and I return the courtesy. A while ago you said you were doing Bright a favor by firing him close to town. I'm doing him a good turn, too. If I were really mad at Bright, I'd let Lukie have him. I'll bet he's more thorough than Buckner." Rod turned his horse toward the distant chuck wagon and kicked him to a trot.

Win's horse pulled abreast, and his voice carried a

laugh when he said, "Just so you'll know, Sweetbean said he'd keep an eye on Monk, too. He's looking forward to it."

"You were real worried over whether I'd approve of firing that swine, weren't you? Already got it set up with Buckner."

Win's chuckles carried easily over the hoofbeats of both their horses and the nearby herd. "I figured you'd back my play, but you wouldn't need to do anything if Buckner was ready. I don't mind stepping back. We'll see what you can do."

"Tell you what, let him eat before you fire him, Win. No need for you to treat him mean. I'll bet you five dollars he can't hold it down."

"I'll take the bet. You always find some way to cheat, but it'll be worth it."

Rod swung down in front of his tent and handed the reins to Lukie. He ducked his head and whispered, "Bright goes tonight."

Lukie took the reins, smiling and bobbing in his perfect imitation of a slow-witted shuffle butt, and spoke in a loud tone. "Good to see you, Mr. Silvana. I sure hopes you had a fine day, suh." In a whisper he added, "Buckner told me. I laid out your fighting shoes. Don't forget to take off that string tie. That's an old shirt anyway, so don't worry about it."

"Buckner's watching Monk and so is Mill. Don't step in unless you can't avoid it."

A twitch of his neck muscles without head movement was enough to signal Lukie's nod of understanding as he turned away with the horse.

Rod stepped into his tent, whipped off his string tie, and loosened the first button of his white shirt. Perched on his cot, he jerked off his riding boots and laced on his custom-made kangaroo-hide gym shoes from England. A quick glance assured him that Lukie had roughed the soles and rubbed them with resin. An uninformed observer would mistake the footwear for ballet slippers had

they not laced up to cover his ankles. He fastened the flap
of his tent and ran in place for a few seconds, touched his
toes several times and went through a thorough stretching routine. He shadowboxed for three or four minutes.
As soon as sweat began to flow freely, he wiped his face
dry and stepped outside.

He caught Atha's eye as she walked with his empty
plate toward the line of men at the chuck wagon. He
shook his head. She came to him with a concerned
expression. "Aren't you hungry?"

"Not yet, Miss Banks. I don't want to be rude, but
would you please retire now? There may be trouble in a
few minutes. I think you would find it unpleasant."

"What? What's going to happen?"

"Permit me to explain later. Please do what I ask.
Right now."

She laid his plate upside down on his folding table in
front of his tent and walked away. The image of her
startled expression stayed with him for a moment while
he scanned the camp. He located Bright seated with his
back against the spokes of the chuck wagon wheel at the
moment Bright's foot snaked out. Nello, passing by with
a full plate and coffee cup balanced in front of him,
tripped and fell flat. Ten feet away, Monk looked up at
the clatter.

Bright's guffaw drew attention from the other men to
Nello as he rose to his knees, eyeing his spilled cup lying
on its side and his plate upside down in the dust. He
sprang to his feet and faced Bright, rawboned hands
fisted.

Win strolled forward. "Stop right there, Nello."

"But Mr. Mill, did you see that? He—"

"No fighting on this trail drive, Nello. You know the
rules. You need this job?"

Nello stood undecided for a moment, clenching and
unclenching his hands, tight as a banjo string, trembling
like a restrained foxhound. Finally he bent to pick up his
plate and cup.

Bright, still seated, snickered and shoved out a foot again, kicking a spray of dust across the kid's lowered hands and arms. "Damn right he needs this job. Nobody else wants to hire him. He ain't worth wet cow chips."

Win stepped between them, a casual, unhurried movement. "Bright, you're fired."

Bright surged to his feet, face twisted. "You can't fire me, you little bastard. I quit this sorry outfit. Nobody ought to have a Yankee runt for a trail boss and a prissy sissy for an owner. I'm saddling up and heading to town. Gimme my pay."

Rod advanced slowly, clutching his hands together timidly in front of him. He faked a hesitant tone. "Pardon me, but I believe everyone hired on for the entire drive. If you quit or get fired, you have nothing coming. No pay, no horse, nothing."

Bright took a long step forward and grabbed a handful of Rod's shirt. "I been working like a dog for more'n a month. I got pay coming or I'll whip you half to death, you little piss ant. You hear me? A man without a horse ain't nothing, so I'm leaving here on a good horse, too." He jerked Rod back and forth, the sound of the tearing shirt loud in the silent camp.

"Yes, of course." Rod said in his meek voice. He reached into his pocket and pulled out a coin. With a single motion, he dropped the coin in the dust with one hand and struck Bright's fist from his shirt with the other. "A man should get what he's worth. Two bits should cover it, don't you think? No horse. Sorry."

Bright stood for a second or two with his jaw slack in astonishment. The timid voice he heard didn't match the words, and he blinked and frowned, trying to make sense of it. Rod decided to help him with a derisive little smirk. Bright finally caught the fact that he was being baited and reached for Rod with a snarl.

Rod's smirk never changed as he stepped to his left, grabbed Bright's extended right arm above the elbow with his left hand, jerked the arm aloft, and pressed

forward. Off balance and unprepared, Bright staggered
back helpless against the pressure of Rod's body until he
crashed against the chuck wagon wheel, turned half
around. Standing beside Bright, Rod sank three vicious
right hooks into his body before the astonished man
could figure a defense. Body pressed against the wheel,
Bright took the full force of the blows. Rod struck him in
the same place each time, precisely at the lower rib
covering the liver. Each blow brought a grunt of pain as
Bright tried without leverage to jerk away and double up,
but he couldn't break the crushing grip on his arm.
Involuntarily, when the first punch struck him, his right
knee came up in his frantic effort to protect his body.

When Bright tried to use his weight to pull away and
drop to the ground, Rod suddenly went with him, jerking
downward on the arm he'd been holding aloft. At the
same time Rod drove his foot into the side of the man's
leg, buckling his knee and driving it into the dust. With
his foot planted in the bend of the knee, Rod pinned
Bright's leg to the ground. He released Bright's right arm
and grabbed his hair, jerked his head back, and chopped
him in the throat. When his hands rose to protect the
throat, Rod struck again at the ribs. Bright's screams of
pain came with the inarticulate sound of a wounded
animal.

When the arm came down to try to protect the ribs, he
jerked Bright's head back and struck the throat again.
Then Rod pushed him forward with both hands. Bright's
head crashed against the spokes of the wagon wheel,
once, twice, three times. Rod, still gripping a handful of
hair, jerked him away from the wagon out into open
space and stepped away. He walked casually in a circle
around the gagging, choking Bright. He lay facedown,
making no attempt to rise. Vomit mixed with blood
spurted from Bright's wide mouth as he tried desperately
to breathe.

Rod continued to stroll in a tight circle around the
downed man, mimicking a casual ramble while he

maintained perfect kicking distance. He was confident the contest was over. He figured it had taken less than ten seconds, start to finish. Quite satisfactory. The only question remaining now was whether Bright would live.

He'd held back on the blows to the neck, but the man's ability to breathe might be lost too long, his throat too paralyzed to recover in time for him to survive. However, if he recovered too strongly or too quickly, Rod planned to kick him into submission. For him, the tense part of the contest had passed. He felt confident Bright had at least one broken rib. Taken completely by surprise, the slow-witted fool had lost the contest before he comprehended it had started.

Then Rod noticed the holstered pistol still resting forgotten on the man's hip. He plucked it out and pitched it to Win. Win spoke in his flat, matter-of-fact tone. "Never saw a man whipped any quicker or better. Never saw a man used for a hammer on a wagon wheel before."

Rod continued his stroll, circling the downed man again and again. He wanted to stay loose, and he wanted to keep his opponent under his eye from all angles. "Gamblers don't like to hit people in the head, Win. You can hurt your hands that way, you know."

It took about five minutes for Bright's breathing to return to nearly normal, but Rod knew it seemed like half an hour to the watching crew. For a while his face had turned a frightening blue, but his normal coloring slowly returned. The men now on shift with the herd would get an earful. They would hate having missed the whole show. Most men enjoyed watching a bruising fight and would rush to see it if they could.

At last Bright sat up. He absently brushed vomit and mud from his face and shirtfront like a man more asleep than awake. After a few moments his watery gaze lifted to meet Rod's. Rod stopped circling while their eyes held for a few seconds. Bright shook his head to the unspoken question and sank back down. He curled up with his knees under his chin, both hands holding his throat.

Rod searched out Monk, standing slouched in the gathering shadows of evening. Monk held out both hands when their eyes met, palms toward Rod. "I warned him, Mr. Silvana. He didn't listen."

"You want to stay or go with him?"

"I signed on for the drive, so I'm staying, Mr. Silvana. I rode with him for a while, but I didn't marry him. Truth to tell, he was wearing on me too."

Win clapped his hands together to draw attention, glanced around, and said, "Eat up, men. I want to head north at moonrise, and there's still half the crew to feed." He unloaded Bright's pistol, reached down and emptied the loops on the motionless man's gun belt, and then shoved the weapon back into its holster. Stuffing the cartridges into a pocket with one hand, he gestured toward Buckner with the other. "Saddle up and take another man with you. Walk Bright here about a mile back toward Fort Worth."

Buckner said, "I'm saddled. Don't need help, boss. Let's go, Bright." Bright came to his knees but buckled forward and heaved. The retching noises from the crouched man seemed to break the other men from a frozen stillness. They turned away, and normal camp movement and clatter resumed. Buckner said sympathetically, "Getting chopped down like that by a sissy sure can make a man sick, can't it, Bright? Come on, it's time to go. You can puke and walk at the same time."

Rod returned to his tent, washed his face and hands, put on a clean shirt, and changed back into his riding boots. When he stepped outside again, Atha stood beside his table. "Are you ready to eat now?"

"Yes, thank you."

A moment later, she put his filled plate in front of him and pulled one of his chairs up close. "Give me the shirt you were wearing. I'll try to mend it for you. You're a surprising man."

"Most men are surprising, Miss Banks, until you get to

know them. Thank you, but never mind the shirt. I do not wear mended garments."

Win walked up and dropped money on Rod's table. "There's the five I owe you. I knew I was throwing it away." He tipped his hat to Atha and turned away.

Rod struggled against a shaky feeling deep inside, an inner trembling. It often troubled him for a while after facing a tense or violent situation, like the wobble of a spinning top as it slowed. He wished she had picked some other time to pass the time of day. His tension didn't show, of that he was confident, but sometimes he couldn't conceal an unstable voice, a tendency to stutter.

"Most men don't come up with your kind of surprises, Mr. Silvana."

He ignored her. He didn't want her to trap him into feeling he needed to justify himself. He cleared his throat and took a sip of coffee. He'd give five dollars for a swallow or two of cool, sweet water, but he might as well have wished for a bite of clean, white snow. Most of the water out here tasted like mud. No wonder the men drank coffee all the time.

"Somehow I didn't picture you doing something like you just did, Mr. Silvana."

"I hoped to spare you an unpleasant sight. I expected you to retire as I requested. I expect all the people who work for me to do what I ask."

There. That should do it. If she had taken the notion the other day he was trying to buy her favors, that pompous comment should set her back. He'd prefer she see him as an arrogant swine than as a socially awkward clod who had to buy attentions from women. Sometimes a man had to settle for the least worst impression he could make when anything better fell beyond his reach.

She didn't blink, simply ignored his response. "You and Mr. Mill set a trap, didn't you? You even made bets."

"Miss Banks, how could we do that?" Rod picked up his fork and examined his plate. "We couldn't know that man would pull a mean trick like that on Nello this evening." If he lived to finish this trail drive, he vowed to himself he'd never eat fried corn bread, beans, and salt pork again if he lived to be a hundred. He stared at his plate with disgust.

He'd give ten dollars right now for a decent cup of shrimp gumbo. Maybe his stomach would relax in another couple of minutes. "Mr. Mill just lost his patience with a troublesome employee causing friction among the crew. I must stand behind him when he makes decisions of that nature."

She rose without answering and walked toward the chuck wagon. Rod breathed a sigh of relief. For the life of him, he couldn't figure why she made him so nervous. Maybe it had something to do with the straight-on look she had. She focused like a rifle, both eyes trained right at his face, like a cat about to jump. Damn! She'd just poured herself a cup of coffee and was coming right back.

She settled herself in the chair again, showing every sign of complete comfort, like she owned the surrounding land. "I realize you don't have to, but I'd like to ask, most respectfully, if you could do me a wonderful favor."

Sensing a trap, he hesitated. "I suppose so. Go ahead, Miss Banks."

"Please don't be angry with me. I promise to be absolutely dependable. I shall never violate your confidence, but I'd like to ask you to stop lying to me."

Back to that again. He put down his fork gratefully. Now he had a good excuse to lose his appetite. She couldn't leave that subject alone. No man could digest anything under this kind of strain, an insult about as direct as a sharp stick in the eye. Still, she'd caught him red-handed once, so it was his own fault. Sometimes a single mistake can dog a man's life without hope for relief. He rubbed his hands together and tried to give himself a moment to compose an answer.

She didn't allow it. She went right on. "You want to be a kind person, but you act like there's something un-manly about it and try to cover it up. You're very strong, and you work very hard to stay physically fit, but your dress and mannerisms are carefully planned to make people think you're a weakling. Everything you do is a cover-up and a lie. I think you're a gentleman, Mr. Silvana, but you have strange pretensions. Why do you act this way?"

He cleared his throat and sat back. He almost had time to say something, but not quite.

"You and Mr. Mill trapped that awful Mr. Bright. I think you decided to fire him because he's been so mean to Nello. Nello's still just a boy, and you don't like to see someone bully him. I think you decided to beat that man up, you planned it in advance. Why don't you just say so, just admit it? After all, you're the owner here. Nobody's going to say you can't do what you want."

Rod leaned forward, determined to speak slowly. He would not rush. If she interrupted, he'd just clam up and to hell with it. He'd maintained his privacy on board ships at sea and on riverboats. He'd kept his distance from curious people in crowded hotels and isolated inns, but he saw now that privacy on a cattle drive was simply impossible.

He spoke deliberately, like a judge instructing a jury from the bench. "Mr. Mill and I planned to fire Bright. He was riding Nello and he made remarks about you, unflattering remarks, remarks sure to cause trouble, maybe get someone killed. He was a poor worker. He complained all the time. He was becoming a source of bad feeling among the men. Besides, I think Mr. Mill took a personal dislike to the man. I do not require Mr. Mill to keep men on the payroll he dislikes."

He stopped and waited, but she said nothing.

"We didn't figure we could fire him without him blowing up and spouting off. That stunt he pulled on Nello tonight was a surprise, but it fit into our plan. We were ready. We felt obliged to make an example of him."

He stopped again, but she didn't say a word.

"I pretend to be a weakling because if trouble comes it

gives me the advantage of surprise. You saw it work against Bright tonight."

She nodded.

"Thank you for not interrupting, Miss Banks." Good. Finished. Now if she presumed to offer unacceptable criticism, by heaven, he'd have her escorted to Fort Worth and be free of her. He had to conduct business ruthlessly, if necessary, but too much rode on the outcome to risk indecision.

"You're welcome, Mr. Silvana. Are you finished?" At his nod, she asked, "Do you suppose we could be friends?"

Braced for criticism, he almost blurted a sharp reply. Instead, he lifted both hands in surprise and spoke before he could stop himself. "I'd be honored, Miss Banks."

His father would have frozen in astonishment at her question, a trace of contempt implied in an otherwise disinterested expression. A friend among the hired help? Indeed not. But then he might slowly nod approval. Rod's response merely met the requirement of gentlemanly discourse with a woman of good character, a mild retort to avoid offense.

But she never had seemed like hired help. Rod couldn't exactly put her in a proper status. Maybe that's why she made him uncomfortable. People out here didn't fit into obvious classes like in New Orleans or Europe.

She leaned forward. "You always seem so tense and formal. If you don't have to lie, maybe you can relax. Tell me, what would you have done if it had gone wrong, if Mr. Bright had turned the tables and beat you up tonight?"

A strangled burst of laughter jerked both of them around to see Lukie Freeman step around Rod's tent. Lukie gave a little bow and said, "Pardon me, but I just happened to be coming to polish Mr. Silvana's boots, and I couldn't help hearing that."

Lukie stood behind Rod, leaned over him with a hand on his shoulder, and spoke in a whisper. "Miss Banks, a

big, awkward country thug matched against an athlete—
trained by the best coaches money can buy, in the best
gymnasiums in America and Europe—has no chance at
all. Just none at all."

She smiled up at Lukie and said, "I wondered why it
looked so easy."

Lukie said, "You have a good eye, ma'am." His grip
tightened on Rod's shoulder. "I suspect you ruptured his
liver. You popped him pretty good. Hurt me, and I was
twenty feet away. He might just bleed to death inside and
die out there in the dark. I hated to see you grab him by
the hair, but you always remember to wash your hands
before you eat, so I didn't worry too much. You want me
to get your boots now?"

Rod didn't look up. "Go away. The lady and I are
talking."

"I guess nobody's going to see your dirty boots while
we ride all night. Good night, folks."

Her smile widened. "Good night, Lukie."

When Rod said nothing, Lukie tightened the hand on
his shoulder and shook gently as if to awaken him. Rod
said, "Go away," without looking up. Lukie chuckled and
ambled off.

"You're wonderful friends, aren't you?" she asked.

"Yes. We've always been together. Always."

"That sounded sincere, like it was the truth." Her voice
carried a note of wonder, of gently teasing encourage-
ment.

Rod stared out into the gathering darkness for several
seconds. He never glanced her way, and he spoke so
softly he heard the whisper of movement when she had
to lean forward to hear him. "Lukie was born on the same
day as I. That's why my father bought him for me,
probably just on an impulse. Lukie's father died before
he was born, and his mother didn't survive his birth." Rod
stopped and took a deep breath. When she let the pause lie
unbroken between them, he continued.

"Once, I guess when we were about ten or twelve, my

father handed me a razor strop. Lukie had misbehaved in some childish way I have forgotten. Probably he spoke to me without respect, and my father overheard, a habit I regret Lukie still has when we are alone." At her look of surprise, he allowed himself a smile. Her expression verified Lukie's discretion. She had heard none of that.

"Anyway, he was my slave, my personal property like my other toys. My father told me I must take responsibility for his conduct, and I must punish him. I tried. I could not."

She continued to lean forward, and he knew she kept her eyes fixed on his face, but he found he couldn't look at her.

"My father is a loving and generous man, Miss Banks, but he's also a rigid, stern man of violent passion."

Her silence, an attentive stillness, became a curiously sympathetic invitation to continue.

"He took the razor strop from me and I saw terrible rage in his eyes. He said, 'If you cannot do your duty, you must be punished. A man without a proper sense of duty is like a ship without a rudder.' He struck me across the face with the strop. Lukie screamed and flew at my father like a furious little black cat. Hit him in the face. Bloodied my father's lip. A slave struck the master of the Silvana house and brought blood."

Rod closed his eyes, a foolish effort to block the picture in his mind, knowing she saw his involuntary shudder. When he glanced at her, one of her hands covered her mouth, her eyes wide in a tense face.

"My father dropped the razor strop and stood perfectly still for a long, long time, eyes narrowed, crouched in a fighting stance, staring at us. His pocket pistol had appeared in his hand like some kind of magic. I have never seen my father other than completely dressed, every button buttoned, every hair in place. I have never seen him in a dressing gown or other informal attire, nor have I ever seen him unarmed. We stood staring back at him, Lukie and I side by side, expecting him to kill us both. In the Silvana house, Miss Banks, one might defy God and be forgiven but never my father.

"Finally, he straightened and said, 'Some things surprise me when they turn out better than I planned. After this, you can never expect me to treat you like children again. Are you that eager to be men so soon?'

"Both of us were too afraid to answer. We stood like statues while he straightened his coat, put a handkerchief to his lip, and left the room. He never offered us a child's punishment after that day. He always spoke and acted toward us like we were men."

Atha leaned forward and spoke softly. "That's the most terrible and yet the most wonderful story I've ever heard. Your father sounds like a perfectly fascinating man."

When she settled back, Rod found himself smiling. He felt a flow of relaxed comfort mixed with a startled awareness that he'd never spoken of that day to another human being. How odd, and yet how natural it seemed. "I think I'm beginning to enjoy your company, Miss Banks."

"I'm thrilled and flattered, Mr. Silvana."

For the first time, her direct gaze didn't trouble him. He found it appealing. In fact, he thought he saw a trace of admiration in her eyes, a fleeting expression in which he took enormous satisfaction.

"If you don't mind tarrying awhile, we could talk a bit more, Miss Banks."

"I'll get us both a fresh cup of coffee."

FOURTEEN

HIRAM REDBONE STARED at the fat man and let silence fall in the camp while he did his own thinking. His scouts had reported the Cowan herd had come across the Red River more than a week ago. Cowan rode for Milt Baynes nowadays, according to rumor, but the drovers were still Cowan's old crew.

Caleb Cowan had been around a long time and had a chilling reputation. There was a story from years back about a tinhorn lawman who shot one of Cowan's men. The lawman ended up hanging from a tree one dark night in front of his burning house. Besides, his crew were all Mexicans, regular hands, no new hires, born in the saddle and loaded down with the best guns to be bought. A man would do about as well attacking a Mexican army unit. Redbone wanted no part of that bunch.

This fat man, calling himself Furnam, had his eye on the same herd Redbone had picked, bossed by a little redheaded former Yankee cavalry officer who had paid cash money to buy cattle all over south Texas. The

Yankee had hired drovers from wherever he could find them, most of them hardly more than boys. But Furnam said that Milt Baynes rode with this bunch rather than his own herd. Bad news, if true, but it didn't make sense. Why would Baynes ride with somebody else rather than his own crew? Furnam said the real owner of most of the cattle was a tenderfoot gambler, not the Yankee.

That came as a surprise. Redbone had figured the Yankee named Mill to be the owner, but it didn't make any difference. Some investors from as far away as Scotland and England speculated in cattle. Bright and Monk could tell him all he needed to know as soon as the herd came close enough for them to see his signal fires. That's when he'd get enough information to know whether to hit them or pick another herd.

Milt Baynes came from Louisiana, not far from Hiram's old home. Too many stories went around about that Baynes family. If half the tales riding the wind were true, they were pure poison, tested gunmen one and all, outlaws really, even though they didn't show up on any Wanted posters he'd seen. This might not shape up as easy as it had looked at first if that Baynes clan took a hand. Some reputations got puffed up out of little or nothing, but Redbone felt sure this one had been written in real blood. It might be smarter to wait and pick another herd, even after all his planning. Still, having a couple of inside men to spook the remuda and put the drovers afoot was a big advantage.

Furnam couldn't stand the quiet, so he started running his mouth again while Redbone tried to think through what he'd learned. With half an ear, Redbone heard something that caught his attention, and he felt his men grow still. He looked up at Furnam and asked sharply, "What was that?"

Furnam drew back and swallowed. The whole camp had gone motionless and silent, everyone staring at him. Redbone waited for him. He'd long known the effect his scarred face and surly disposition had on some men.

Furnam gulped again and said, "I was just talking about a fellow who came into Fort Worth while I was there—he staggered in late one night. Everybody was talking about it. The doctor said it looked like a horse kicked him in the belly and tore him up inside. He passed out in the street before he said a word."

"Didn't I hear you say his name?"

"Yeah, they asked all around to see if anybody knew him. Said they found papers on him made the sheriff think he might be named Clete Bright." Furnam's eyes jerked around as his gaze jumped from one to another of Redbone's five men, all standing now in tense silence. The three other men who had ridden in with Furnam wore tight expressions, obviously wondering what had brought on the rigid stillness.

Redbone looked at one of his men. He got a nod and a laconic comment, "That was Clete Bright that rode with Monk, Hiram. That must be him."

"Nobody with Bright, Furnam?"

Furnam shook his head, avoiding Redbone's one-eyed gaze.

This deal was turning sour before it even got started. Without Monk and Bright on the inside, his plan turned into smoke and wind. Redbone turned his gaze to Furnam. "I don't need you, but I might cut you in. I'll ponder on it for a while. There's only one boss here, though. You agree to that or ride on."

Furnam nodded. "As long as you hit this herd, I'm with you. I got my reasons."

Redbone commented flatly, the words not directed at anyone in particular, "I'm not liking a man lost before we even make a move. Not a good sign. Bright didn't stack high to my eye, but he was riding with Monk, so he was one of us." He waved at Furnam's men. "Unsaddle and rest yourselves, men."

If Bright got hurt doing his job, his trail boss wouldn't have sent him to town alone and hurting. Redbone wondered if Bright's mouth had got him in Dutch. He'd shown too much mouth in his short stay in the Redbone camp, but Monk tolerated him. If somebody had whipped him good to get information from him, Monk would have found an excuse to stop it if he could. That might mean Monk had had to expose himself too. No way to know anything until the herd came closer. If Monk came to the signal fire, good. Otherwise, maybe they could still swing it with surprise alone. Nothing to do but wait. No need to move until the herd got a lot closer to Abilene.

FIFTEEN

ROD REINED IN beside Lukie's wagon and rode for a while without saying anything. Finally he said, "You're full of talk today."

Lukie looked up with a smirk. "Nothing to talk about. I haven't seen a single house or a living human soul since we crossed the Red River two weeks ago. I learned something when we crossed that picturesque landmark. I didn't know red mud moved downstream almost the same as water, and I didn't know people could be tricked into calling it a river. Shows how dumb people out here must be, except there aren't any people out here."

"I never found you short of something to blow about before."

Lukie's derisive grin widened. "I been trying to leave you alone to give your mouth a rest. You've been talking so much to that woman the last two or three weeks you must have a sore throat. Didn't figure you'd have breath left for me."

Rod heaved a disgusted groan and looked away.

"Shaping up into a sweet trail drive romance, you two sitting around giggling and talking every evening for a couple of hours." Lukie glanced up with wide-eyed innocence. "You plan on wrapping her up and taking her home with us?"

"Don't be silly."

"Nothing silly about me. We're talking about you. You're sinking in quicksand, going down fast."

"Nonsense."

"Rod, I told you I like that woman, but you're getting in trouble. Her kind makes the worst taffy bear in the world."

"What're you talking about?"

"Taffy bears. Touch one and it'll stick to you every time. They're pure hell to shake loose."

"Don't be vulgar. I'm not touching anybody. We just talk. She's good company."

Lukie nodded solemnly. "Most all taffy bears are wonderful company, makes them stickier."

"You see me taking her home to meet my father?" Rod shifted in the saddle, taken aback by his own serious tone.

Lukie sat on the wagon seat with his eyes fixed straight forward. When he didn't answer, Rod said, "Well?"

"You're in deeper than I thought. I'm thinking on it." He rode for several minutes without showing any intention to continue the conversation.

Finally Rod said, "I guess silence can be a good enough answer."

"Not near good enough." Lukie rubbed his nose and shifted on the wooden seat as if bracing himself to lift something heavy. "Your father probably figures you'll pick a woman from a fancy family. He probably expects you to pick somebody who brings both money and property to the deal. He'd probably like that. I keep saying 'probably.' Predicting him is a crazy gamble. How many times have you ever felt sure you knew what he might be thinking?"

"A few."

"Were you right?"

"Not always."

"So it takes some thinking before coming up with a guess about how he might react. She has pretty manners, even makes herself pleasant to poor little ex-slaves, and she talks good English. That all she speaks?"

"Never heard her speak any other language. Never had occasion to ask."

"Me neither. Want me to ask her?"

Rod pointed an accusing finger. "You leave her alone. You blabbed your head off to her enough, told her everything you knew about me. I think you made up a bunch of crap that got her interested. I still haven't made up my mind whether or not to kick your butt for that."

Lukie lifted an innocent palm. "I just told her you were rich and spoiled, and rich and arrogant, and rich and nearly helpless without me."

Rod stared at him. "You're so rotten I can smell you clear over here. Just had to do it, didn't you?"

Lukie kept his eyes straight ahead. "Yeah, because she asked. Impatient woman. Wants to know about things. If she'd waited two or three days more she wouldn't have needed to ask anyhow. She could have seen all that for herself. I never told that white woman anything but hand-on-the-Bible truth. If she got interested in you, that's her mistake, not mine. I'm taking no blame for it. Not even one little, tiny bit. Besides, I'm disappointed. I thought she had better judgment."

"You blabbed about me being rich. You think she's after money?" Rod tensed as he posed the question. Lukie had lived a lifetime of watching white people from the corners of his eyes. His opinions seldom missed the mark.

"Why, hell yes, Rod. I only said I like her. I didn't say she was different from everybody else in the world. Aren't we after money too? Why else are we out here in the middle of this endless, dusty, cow-stink paradise? I thought it was for money. Maybe you like it out here. Did I miss something? Did you lose your mind and I didn't notice?"

Rod leaned forward and grinned into a hot pair of eyes. The tone of Lukie's voice had gone from banter to anger in a flash. The implication that Atha might be a gold-digging woman had clearly riled him. "You really do like her, don't you?"

"Damn right. She acts like she's fond of you, but otherwise she's smart as hell. She's not afraid to work, and she tries to please. Those aren't the kinds of things a smart man laughs and jokes about. Besides, she's about as good looking as a white woman can get. You need to find somebody soon or you'll never settle down. You're already cranky and set in your ways. I don't know, though. A woman of good character might rip you to pieces if you try to get too close. She'll likely kick your silly white ass over the moon."

"You want me to settle down, Lukie?"

An answering grin flickered across the black man's features. Grudgingly he nodded. "Wouldn't be a bad thing. You're about ready to act like a grown man."

A suspicion struck Rod like a blow and straightened him in the saddle. "What's her name?"

Lukie swung his gaze straight forward again and didn't answer. Rod settled patiently in the saddle and rode for over ten minutes in silence. Finally a muttered response came.

"Melinda."

"Where is she, Lukie?"

"New Orleans." His mumbled response sounded more like "Narlens."

"She waiting for you?"

Lukie shrugged and spoke in an offhand manner.

"Yeah. I told her I got you to look after. I got responsibilities, you being near helpless without me. Couldn't let you come out here and get kicked to death by a milk cow or something. Said she'd wait, but she doesn't want any here-today, gone-tomorrow man. When we get home, I think I better put up or shut up."

"For heaven's sake, why didn't you tell me?"

"You'd just worry yourself about it. You're a terrible worrier. Like right now. Hell, Rod, you haven't even asked that Atha girl. Your little orphan girl hasn't had her chance to say yes or go to hell yet, and you're fretting yourself into a fever. You're already worrying yourself into a nervous puddle about facing your daddy. You better worry about what she says before worrying about him."

"I guess you're right, Lukie. I've been toying with the idea like testing a hot iron with a wet finger. If I decide to ask her, and she says yes, I guess you'll want to stand up with me, back me up when I talk to my father, help me out with that."

Another long silence fell. After a few minutes, Lukie squinted up at Rod and said quietly, "That will be a good time for a fine, upstanding young man of color to be far away from the Silvana house. Clear across town. A mile. Yeah. I'll want to be at least a mile away from your daddy, hidden under a table in a dark corner, with lookouts posted and a fast horse close by." He leaned far out, stretched a long arm, and grabbed Rod's knee with a paralyzing grip. "Your daddy might want to shoot a man or two just to blow off steam and clear his mind."

Rod laughed and reined aside to break the powerful grip, nearly unseating himself in the process. "Never mind. You may have to take the risk."

He rode beyond Lukie's reach for a while before he added, "I want to meet your Melinda and tell her about you. It'll take me all day, and I'm going to love every minute of it. Most of all, I'll tell her not to tell you to put up or shut up. You may put up or you may not, but there's no chance in this life you'll ever shut up."

Lukie wiped his mouth but failed to conceal his grin. "She already knows you're the biggest liar in the world. I'm not worried."

SIXTEEN

MILT RODE A lathered horse up beside Rod and said, "I had a hard time finding you. Been out riding by yourself?"

"Yeah. Doing some thinking."

"Get on a fresh horse quick as you can. Win's warning the crew. He'll send more men to look after the remuda. Whatever happens, he doesn't want us afoot. I think we got trouble coming."

They rode together back to the remuda. Rod followed suit while Milt jerked the saddle off his tired mount and threw a loop over his scarred old mustang, the vicious Judas. Without comment, Milt coiled his rope again and flipped it over the head of Rod's long-legged night horse. Rod still hadn't learned to throw a rope worth a damn. Lukie, of course, had seemed to learn after about three tries, and now he flipped rope with the best of the trail hands.

Milt kept talking, his happy smile that of a man about to ride to a barn dance. "Figured I'd better come get my

war horse. Judas hasn't smelled gunpowder for so long
he thinks something's wrong with his nose. I been
watching eight or ten men. They've been moving along
with us for several days, thinking they're out of sight.
Before that, they stayed in the same camp doing nothing
for more than a week. That makes no sense to me unless
they're up to mischief. Somebody from our crew rode
out and met up with them last night. Didn't have time to
find clean tracks, so I don't know who or why, so watch
your back. They're heading our way. It sure enough
looks like trouble."

"Why didn't you say something before?"

"No point unless they moved to crowd us. Why make
everybody edgy?"

"You don't look unhappy about it."

Milt paused, hand on the pommel of his saddle. All
sign of haste vanished now that Judas stood ready.
"Cousin, I still have a lot to learn before I become the
best cattleman in the world, but trouble I'm good at.
Everybody likes to do what he's good at."

He vaulted into the saddle without touching his
stirrups. "Win's telling his boys to fire warning shots. If
they keep coming, he's telling our men to shoot for their
horses first and at men only if necessary. If the cattle run
and things get mixed up, he wants everybody to be
careful we don't shoot at each other."

Rod slid his rifle from its boot and checked the loads.
"Sounds good to me. What if they mean no harm?"

"Texans don't have a friendly reputation in these parts
anyhow. Don't worry about a little gunpowder rudeness.
Win gives orders to everybody but you and me, Cousin.
Me, now, I don't shoot at horses." Milt laughed and
spoke over his shoulder as Judas moved forward at a
sedate walk. "Be sure the teams are hitched up, but don't
move the wagons unless you're forced to it. Otherwise,
stay here so the boys know where to come for help if
somebody gets hurt. Look sharp. If strangers try to
approach the camp, start shooting. They'd like nothing

better than to get in close and surprise us. Do I need to tell you Win expects you and Lukie to look after Atha?"

"Why don't we ride out to meet those men? Maybe we could head them off before they get close to the herd."

Milt raised his voice as Judas carried him farther away. "They were splitting up when I had my last peep at them, but they were all pointed this way. They looked like they're going to come at us all spread out."

Rod mounted slowly. The more he thought about it, the more he felt blood rise to his face. His own cousin evidently never gave a thought to the implied insult, but Rod suffered a slow burn. Milt's easy tones came back to him, telling story after story in the evenings from his seat in the shadows away from the firelight. Milt admired the Plains Indians and their habits. They left old men, wounded warriors, cripples, and young boys behind to guard the women and children in their camps when war parties rode out to face trouble. Rod turned his horse toward the nearby wagons, grimly trying to control his anger.

All right, he'd guard the camp and the lone woman among them. Among these men, he remained a tenderfoot. Maybe they treated all owners this way. Maybe they feared for their wages if the owner got hurt. Besides, he knew his city manners brought on the same amusement among these men as a country person's awkwardness did among city people.

The cook already had the evening fire going, and everything looked normal except for the holstered pistol on his usually bare hip. A prominent bulge in the front of the man's apron signaled another pistol stuck under his belt, and a rifle leaned against the larder box near at hand. While Rod watched, the cook made a casual circuit around the cooking fire as if checking to see if it burned evenly, but his gaze lifted often to sweep the prairie all around the camp.

When Rod drew near, the cook greeted him with a grin. "We'll likely have cattle running everywhere pretty soon, boss. I've seen this kind of trouble before. Main-most thing we got to do is hang onto the horses and this here food. Our boys won't do no good gathering scattered cattle back up unless they got horses to ride and a bite to eat now and again."

"Yeah, you're right. I guess you're just about the most important man in the bunch." Rod used a joshing tone, but the response came with open sincerity.

"Yessir, that's the way I figure it too. That's why I asked Mr. Mill for double wages when I hired on, and I reckon that's why he didn't give me no back talk. Mr. Mill don't waste no breath on dumb gab. He's one of them smart Yankees. Don't run into smart Yankees much, so when you bump into one it pays to take notice."

"What about the horses? I just came from there, but I didn't think about it. Shouldn't they be closer to us?"

"That Banks kid's going to bring them up. He's going to tie them horses together on a long tether before dark. Even if they bust loose running, they can't scatter, and they can't go nowhere fast. Since they got to stay together, he can stay with the bunch without straining himself. That youngster ain't no dummy neither."

"He was by himself when I left him a few minutes ago. Is anybody going to give him any help?"

"Sweetbean Buckner's going to be riding in with a couple of the other boys. He's a shooter, Mr. Silvana. Anybody bothers the horses, Sweetbean's going to burn powder. You can lay a bet on that. He shoots first and gets pious later. As for your nigger, he hasn't got more'n three feet from Miss Banks since Mr. Baynes spread the word we might have trouble. Looks like he'd like to hide behind her skirt."

"His name is Lukie Freeman."

"Will that boy stand, Mr. Silvana?"

Rod stared off into the distance, eyeing the empty prairie for a moment before he answered. He decided lying to one of his own men made no sense anymore. Pretense had no place when dealing with men willing to face gunfire to protect his property. "Miss Banks will be the safest one out here if there's trouble. Even if everybody else starts to buckle and run, look for him to fold last."

The cook spat to the side. "I ain't surprised."

"I'd be obliged if you'd call him Freeman rather than 'my boy' or 'my nigger.'"

"I got your drift, Mr. Silvana. My pa used to say there's nothing more dangerous than a polite man when he's riled up. Maybe he had somebody like Freeman in mind when he taught me to be careful thataway."

"Dumb mistakes are always the hardest to live with."

"Yessir, a man could be embarrassed plumb to death."

Rod faced the man directly, openly searching his face. "You knew the answer about Freeman before you asked, didn't you?"

"Yessir, I had it figured. Just wondered if you'd level with me. I saw him checking his pistol over behind your wagon. He ain't the least bit awkward with that thing when he don't think anybody's looking. He caught me looking at him and gave me a grin like a possum eating yellow jackets. I think I got you figured too."

"That so?"

"I got to say you play it close to the vest, pretending to be a sissy like you do. Most men try to act tough, but you play that game backwards. Took all of us quite a while to catch on. Everybody thinks it's a neat trick, and you carry it off real good."

"Well, uh, thanks, I guess. You know, after all this time, I don't know your name. You're just listed on the payroll as Cook."

"Yessir, that's me, Franky Cook, but nobody calls me Franky unless he's looking to get his butt kicked."

"You said you've been through this before. If we have trouble, when's it most likely?"

"Soon after dark, Mr. Silvana. Rustlers don't like getting shot at any more than anybody else. After dark, our boys will be slow to shoot for fear of knocking each other out of the saddle. Mr. Mill told all our boys to sing out, if they're able, if they got to come to the wagons after dark. I know all their voices."

"Makes sense, but it's the first I heard of that."

"No chance. You were off riding around somewhere. Mr. Mill ain't had no chance to get everybody together since Baynes smelled trouble. He probably figured I'd tell you."

"I see."

"You do what you please, boss, but it's a good idea to lie low when it gets dark. We can see a horseman outlined against the sky better than they can see us. I got the wheels on the wagons jammed and chocked with rocks and the reins are tied down. Don't forget to kick that stuff out from under the wheels if we got to make a run. Your man Freeman made a place for Miss Banks under her wagon with flour bags and stuff all around her."

"I think maybe I ought to go see how Miss Banks is doing."

Cook rubbed a hand across his mouth too late to cover a grin. "I fancy she'll take that kindly. Give my regards to your . . . to Mr. Freeman."

Rod led his horse the short distance to Atha's wagon, where she met him with a smile. His shotgun leaning against the sideboard beside her caught his eye. He returned her smile, picked up his shotgun, and broke it open to check the loads. Lukie walked from Rod's wagon to join them. When Rod glanced his way, Lukie assumed an innocent expression.

"I never saw anything so beautiful," Atha said, and ran her hand across the glistening walnut stock. "I didn't even know a gun could be decorated like that."

"I had it custom-made when I spent some time in Spain." He ran a finger along the carved ivory inlay in the stock. "This part was done in China after they seasoned the wood for two years. Then the stock was sent to Spain for final carving and sized to fit me. The barrels were painstakingly silver soldered together by Spanish craftsmen so the shot will cross exactly thirty yards out from the muzzles. The gold and silver engraving was done last, after the weapon passed about a hundred rigid tests."

She stared at him with wide eyes. "It's a masterpiece. I didn't know anybody but royalty could own something like that."

"There aren't many of them. Rare and expensive, they're made only to satisfy people who require the very best. I've used it many times, so I'm confident it's an excellent piece—not just beautiful, but the most dependable and accurate of its kind in the world." He paused for a moment, eyed the weapon from end to end critically, and finally nodded as if satisfied. He offered it to her. "It was made for me, but you're nice and tall. You should be able to use it comfortably. As good as it is, it's barely good enough for you."

Her hands rose to accept the weapon, but she stopped herself and clasped them together. "You sound like you're giving it to me to keep."

"Of course. Just think, someday you'll tell your grandchildren that a nice man gave this to you just hours—maybe just minutes—before you shot a dozen outlaws with it, saved a whole herd of cattle, and protected a bunch of terror-stricken drovers."

"You can't be serious."

"I'm dead serious, if you'll forgive an awful pun." He took her hand, folded her fingers around the barrels, and left the weapon in her hand. "Now, please excuse me, Miss Banks. I need to confer with Lukie."

He left her standing in speechless surprise and motioned to Lukie to follow him. A few steps away, he slowed and spoke in a low tone. "When did I give you permission to dig out my best shotgun?"

"I had to give her something to defend herself." Lukie's tone vibrated with distress. He sounded like he was trying to apologize for shooting Rod by accident.

"She didn't act like she knew anything about a pistol, but she said she knew how to use her brother's shotgun. It seemed like it made sense. I didn't even think she'd have to use it. I thought she'd just feel better having it around. I never dreamed you'd give it away. You love that thing. How could you do that?"

"To teach you a lesson."

"Me? You give away your prized shotgun, and it's supposed to teach me something? Well, it did, I guess, come to think of it. I feel awful."

"You're going to feel worse in just a minute."

"Go ahead. Pop me one. I'll feel better if you do."

"I'll do better than that. I'm going to teach you to stop handing my stuff around. Did you examine it before you handed it over?"

"Didn't have time, Rod. I just pointed to the case, and she dug it out and loaded it herself."

"I just gave her your shotgun."

"What?" Lukie flinched like he'd stepped on a hot coal. "My shotgun? No. You couldn't. Mine's at home in your gun rack."

Rod stopped and laid a hand on Lukie's shoulder. He kept his voice gentle. "I was afraid mine would get scratched on this rough trip, so I brought yours instead. Remember how I got mine with an ivory bead front sight, and you got yours with a ruby? I told you the ruby looked tacky, and you ordering a gun just like mine other than that showed poor taste, but you went into a sulk and insisted on it, didn't you. Go back and admire your ruby bead, Lukie, and save your money. Next time we're in Spain, maybe we can get you another shotgun."

Lukie set his feet and froze. Rod, knowing Lukie had narrowly avoided taking a swing at him, smiled in what he hoped was his most infuriating manner. "How does it feel, having your property passed around without even a howdy-do or a thank you?"

"We get us some privacy, I'm going to punch your lights out. You'll never chew straight again. You won't

have two teeth that meet when I finish with you." Lukie's
fingers curled and straightened a couple of times.

Rod nodded and put on a smug expression. "Good
lesson. Now you know how mad it can make you."

The fierce light went out of Lukie's eyes and he
rubbed his forehead. "Rod, you broke my heart. I
treasured that shotgun. It made me feel like the pharaoh
of Egypt. I never owned anything else in my whole life
that made me feel so big and important."

"Go tell Miss Banks it's yours, and I had no right to
give it away."

Lukie's face twisted. "I couldn't do that."

"Think you're too proud, do you? Come on." Rod
grabbed an arm and pulled Lukie back to Atha's wagon.
"Miss Banks, hand that shotgun to Lukie, will you? He
wants another look at it."

Atha handed it to Lukie, her gaze shifting from one
man to the other, silent curiosity written on her face.

Lukie accepted it, his face stiff, lips in a stern line.
After a murderous glance at Rod, he looked down and
ran a finger along the gleaming stock. Then his eyes
fixed on the front sight and shock loosened his tense
face. "That's not a ruby. That's ivory."

Rod swung into the saddle. "Of course not. A ruby
would look gaudy on a man's gun and tasteless on a
lady's. I'm going over to help those boys move the
horses closer to the wagons."

SEVENTEEN

ROD KNEW THE first shot came from far away, but in the stillness of the night it sounded sharp and clear. Cook's voice, placid and edged with smug humor, came from the shadows near his guttering fire. "Listen at that. Didn't I say so? They're hitting us before the moon rises. What did I tell you, Mr. Silvana?"

Scattered shots came as if to prove his point, the flashes all coming from the eastern flank of the tightly packed herd. Rod couldn't see the animals, but he knew well by now the sound of massed beeves springing to their feet and beginning to mill.

"You called it right, Mr. Cook." Rod sat on the ground beside Lukie next to Atha's wagon. Lukie's rig made a dim outline only ten feet away, on line with Cook's, which stood hidden by darkness another ten feet beyond. Atha sat near Rod's other side on one of his folding chairs. She had pinned up her apron and stuffed ten or twenty shells into the makeshift pocket. The shotgun lay balanced comfortably across her lap, and she idly stroked the polished stock like a pet kitten.

"You might want to settle yourself in the place Lukie made for you, Miss Banks." Rod forced his voice to sound calm. "If you have to shoot, you'll be safer behind something. Those boys might not ordinarily shoot at a woman, but they'll be shooting back at gun flashes."

"I'll not be shooting unless they come very close and force me to defend myself, Mr. Silvana. If that happens, I doubt they'll be up to shooting back."

Lukie chuckled. "Any more advice, Mr. Silvana?"

Atha spoke quickly. "I beg your pardon. I didn't mean to sound snippy."

"Never mind." Rod came to his feet. "I think I'll mount up and ride over to the remuda."

"I think you ought to stay here with Miss Banks." Lukie rose behind Rod and punched him lightly on the shoulder. "You go traipsing around and one of your own employees might shoot at you. Bad for worker discipline. I better sneak over closer to my wagon."

Only a few seconds after Lukie's dim figure blended into the darkness, a bullet tugged at the tail of Rod's coat, smashed through the sideboard of Atha's wagon, and hit something inside with a metallic clang. Rod caught the muzzle flash out of the corner of his eye, dropped to one knee, whipped up his Spencer, and fired three times, one left, one center, one right, holding low. Then he jumped behind the wagon to reload. Gasping with shock at the sudden action, he marveled at Atha's cool question from her new position under the wagon.

"Why don't Lukie and Mr. Cook shoot back too?"

"I think what just happened is what military books I've read call a reconnaissance by fire. They wanted to tempt us to shoot back to find out how many of us are hanging around these wagons and where we are. Lukie read the same books I did, so he didn't shoot back. I guess Mr. Cook learned the same thing the hard way."

"Why did you shoot, then?"

"Because I have a passionate and unstable nature, Miss Banks. I become aroused when someone shoots a hole in an expensive coat of mine."

"Are you hurt?"

"Only my coat and my feelings." The unmistakable rumble of running cattle vibrated through the night. "And, I fear, my pocketbook. There goes the herd."

"What about the horses, Mr. Silvana?"

"If they ran, we'd hear it. It's dead quiet over there."

Rod endured ominous quiet around the wagons. He stood in furious helplessness, listening to his herd run away, with occasional gunshots coming from greater distances. After about twenty minutes of frustration, Rod nearly dropped his Spencer when a voice spoke almost at his elbow. "Don't shoot at kinfolks."

"Damn! You scared me to death, Milt. How did you sneak up on me? Where's Judas?"

"Over yonder eating grass."

"Aren't you afraid those people might run off with him?"

"You want to fool with Judas, Cousin? That'd be bad for me. I'd have to go tell your daddy how my pet horse stomped your dumb head six inches deep into a Kansas prairie."

"Never mind. Where have you been?"

"I followed three men up near here. Figured on snagging one of them and having a chat. Had it in my mind I might learn something. You know how I admire learning, Cousin. Bad luck. One of them fired a shot at the wagons and somebody around here someplace lost his temper, up and drilled him dead center before I could sing 'swing your partner.' The other two lost interest and rode off like their tails were afire. Left the poor devil lying out there before he quit leaking."

"The man died?" Atha's voice drew a startled flinch from Milt.

"Well, now, look who's here." Milt bent to peer under the wagon. "You got you a snug little hidey-hole there,

Miss Banks." He dropped to one knee. "For a minute there, I thought my cousin had started wearing perfume. I was beginning to wonder about him."

"You didn't answer my question."

"Oh. Yes, ma'am, that man surely died. He definitely, absolutely, certainly did. You know, at first, I figured it was Mr. Cook who shot that fellow. He's a man easily irritated, but he's way over yonder, and the shot came from here. Then I figured on Lukie Freeman. He has testy days too, now and then, but he's over yonder as well. I guess you must have shot him, Miss Banks."

"No, no, it was Mr. Silvana."

"Oh, my heavens, not my mild-mannered cousin." Milt's voice gushed fake astonishment, and both his hands flipped up in theatrical amazement.

"You're having a wonderful time, aren't you, Milt, while my whole herd stampedes away as fast as they can run?"

"Don't get the vapors, Cousin Rod. The sun will rise tomorrow morning. We still have a good crew, lots of horses, and a good cook. So far as I know, none of our boys are hurt, but I guess I better go snoop around some more." He cocked his head to listen to the fading sound of gunshots. "Somebody might need some help."

Before Rod could answer, Milt came to his feet and faded into the darkness with an effortless, silent trot.

Atha slid out from under the wagon to stand beside Rod. She touched his arm and asked, "Do you think they'll shoot at the wagons anymore?"

"I don't know, Miss Banks, but I do wish you'd stay under there until it gets light. Would you do that, please?"

Without a word, she stooped and vanished under the wagon. After a long silence she spoke again. "You should have told Milt how close that bullet came, that it went through your coat."

Rod took a deep breath. "Yes, ma'am, you're right. He knows how I like to keep my clothes neat. He'd understand that a ruined coat would make me mad enough to kill somebody, a man I never even saw, maybe a man with a family."

"Why do you always do that, Mr. Silvana?"

"What?"

"Talk like you're such a ruthless and selfish person. You keep doing it, and it's disgraceful. That man was trying to kill you and steal your property. You're a generous and decent man. You had every right to defend yourself."

Rod couldn't come up with an answer, so he stood scanning the darkness, listening with all his might for stealthy movement. Milt had walked right up to him unseen and unheard. That left him feeling shaky inside, and he knew damn well Milt had intended to achieve exactly that reaction. Rod's cousin had a way of making himself clear without saying a single word.

No telling how many of Rod's father's cattle had been lost on this moonless night far from anything familiar. He moved a few silent, restless steps back and forth, both to gain a little relief from tight nerves and to change his viewpoint. Milt had lectured him about how much a man could see sometimes by moving just a few inches that he'd miss otherwise.

He smiled into the pitch-black night and felt a sense of wonder at how little it took to make him feel good even while he was both scared and furious. No telling how much this little adventure tonight had damaged his father's investment. No telling how long the spector of having killed a stranger would haunt him.

Still, he felt good. All it took was a few kind words to lift him from despair, words uttered by a penniless orphan girl from a common, maybe even menial background. She'd spoken in a sharp, impatient, nearly scolding tone, and he savored the sound of it.

Why shouldn't he find her a source of strength? All aristocratic families had lowly beginnings, but many of them disintegrated into disgrace, desperately needing an infusion of robust common blood. She was certainly robust enough.

Besides, he'd best remember she was no longer a waif without assets. She had become a woman of means. She owned an extraordinarily fine shotgun, a treasure of the finest workmanship in the world, worth a considerable sum of money. He felt his secret smile widen, tightening cheeks finally becoming toughened by sun and wind. He had to smother a chuckle, afraid she'd hear him.

"You might as well get some sleep, Miss Banks."

"Wouldn't you like me to talk to you? It might help you stay awake."

"I think it better to let me listen. Milt walked right up on me like I was already asleep. I'll get you a blanket."

"Lukie already put one under here for me, thank you. Good night, Mr. Silvana."

"Good night, Miss Banks."

"The moon's coming up. Look how big and pretty it is."

Rod rolled his eyes and passed a hand across his face before he allowed himself a glance at the rising moon. He'd probably lost a fortune within the last hour, but this woman didn't want him to miss the enjoyment of a clear summer night. She would probably enjoy the beauty of whitecaps in a storm while a boat sunk under her. "Good night, Miss Banks."

EIGHTEEN

ATHA BANKS AWOKE concerned about him and complained that he hadn't woken her so she could have stood a tour of the night-long watch. Rod pointed toward the chuck wagon and pretended to bring a cup to his lips. She fell silent and walked the short distance with him, shotgun cradled in the bend of her elbow with the same casual ease he imagined she would carry a furled parasol.

Rod strolled along beside her suppressing a smile. He had anticipated her complaint, and now he expected the silence. She made her point firmly and then dropped the subject. That was her way, and he expected to hear no more about it. She simply wasn't the kind of woman to repeat herself.

Cook stood over a steaming kettle, nodded a greeting, and filled two cups from the nearby coffeepot. Rod waited as they went through the ritual they had developed. Cook handed Rod's cup to Atha, and she passed it to him. Somewhere along the line the two of them had come to an agreement that Cook prepared the food with her help, but she took care of looking after the boss by herself.

Lukie, slouched against the chuck wagon, gave Rod a wink. "We might as well unhitch the animals and let them graze. Cook says we won't be moving the wagons for a while. The men need to know where we are."

Rod nodded and blew across his steaming cup. He never had mastered the art of drinking coffee that seemed to him still on the edge of boiling. One experience with the lip of the hot tin cup against a tender mouth taught him what drovers meant by the expression "Cool it." Never show impatience. Trying to do any task before the proper time could produce painful results, especially downing a cup of blistering coffee.

"Cook."

"Yeah, boss?"

"Put me up a big bunch of sandwiches."

"Got 'em ready for you. They're in that bag yonder."

"You're thinking ahead of me."

A trace of a smile lived a brief existence on the leathery face. "Didn't take no genius to figure you'd be riding out to snoop around this morning. I figured you might run into some drovers suffering from hollow belly along the way."

"Lukie."

"I'm here."

"Milt said one of the men who shot at us last night caught a bullet and died out there. Would you go find him and put him in the ground?"

"How deep?"

"Whatever you feel is right."

"I'll do it. I got a pretty good idea where he might be. Mark that off your list." He jerked a shovel off his wagon, shouldered it, and strolled away, rifle in his other hand.

The sun had yet to peak over the edge of the prairie when Rod mounted and rode to the remuda. Sweetbean

Buckner sat quietly in the saddle until Rod reined in beside him. "Bad news, Mr. Silvana."

"I know." Rod pulled off his hat and ran his silk handkerchief around the sweatband. "I guess the herd must be scattered all over half the country."

"That ain't what I mean, boss. We still got our horses, so we can round up those critters, at least most of them. I mean one of our own boys was in on this deal."

"What happened?"

"I let him go." Buckner ducked his head and looked away.

Rod settled his hat carefully, stuffed his handkerchief back in his pocket, and looked off into the distance. Buckner sounded belligerent, his angry tone that of an embarrassed man expecting criticism. Prompting him would gain nothing, so Rod sat quietly through a long, tense silence.

"I caught him last night, Mr. Silvana. I rode up to check to be sure that Banks kid was all right. When I left him, I walked over by the horses the kid had strung together, intending to take a leak. I walked right up to Monk before I saw him. He had a blade in his hand, getting ready to cut the horses loose, I reckon."

"You run him off?"

"That ain't exactly the way it went, boss. I didn't really catch on until I found myself looking down the barrel of a gun. Monk says to me, 'I don't want to kill you, Sweetbean,' and I says, 'I ain't so easy to kill, Monk.'"

Buckner pulled off his hat and rubbed his face. "I felt mighty stupid, with all these goings-on, letting myself get caught off guard so easy. He had me cold. Hell, if he hadn't pulled a gun, I don't think I'd even have caught on to what he was up to. Then he says, 'I'm going to get my horse and ride off from here, Sweetbean. I won't shoot you if you'll give me your word you won't shoot me.'"

"I done it, boss. Didn't see no other way. So old Monk just climbed on his horse and rode off. Never looked back, near as I could see. I pulled iron and was sorely tempted, but I couldn't shoot him. I done gave my word I wouldn't. Only good thing about it, boss, is we didn't lose no horses."

"Seems to me you played it smart," Rod said. "I can't see how you could have done anything any better."

Buckner took a long, deep breath. "That's a comfort to me, Mr. Silvana. I didn't know how you'd take it. You know, I always smelled something strange about old Monk, but I liked him. Yes, sir, I did. Maybe it was him partnering with that rotten cow chip called himself Bright that didn't set right with me. Bright was sour enough to draw flies from a day's ride upwind. Them two didn't fit together nohow, but a man can never tell. I've seen some strange partners paired up in my day."

"You tell anybody else yet?"

"No, sir. Wait, I did too. I told Nello. But we ain't seen none of the other boys since the herd went to running."

"I'll spread the word. No need for any of our other boys to face the same surprise you had if we can help it. Rig five or six horses to a lead line for me to take with me. I'll be back in a minute. I'm going to send Nello in for some sleep. You'll have to look after the horses by yourself for a while." Buckner nodded and yawned, just to show how thrilled he was to spend a few more hours in the saddle without rest.

Rod rode around to the other side of the remuda, lifted a hand in greeting to Nello Banks, and said, "Ride over and tell your sister you're all right. Get a bite to eat and a couple hours' sleep." The boy's angular features, drawn with fatigue, brightened at the prospect. He turned his horse at once and loped toward the wagons. By the time Rod rode back to Buckner, the horses were ready.

The shredded ground offered no challenge to trailing the cattle from their last bed ground. Rod, leading six horses, rode with his back to a rising sun that announced itself like hot bricks pressed against his shoulder blades.

The tracks didn't tell the story he expected to read on the ground. He anticipated the animals would take off in every direction possible, but they didn't. It looked like most of the herd stayed together, running on a broad front instead of in the usual long column. Easing along at a gentle pace to save the horses, he rode for an hour before he saw the first cattle, and they were heading back toward him. He circled wide and soon spotted two drovers riding drag.

As soon as they saw him, their mounts turned his way. The first to draw near, a rawboned, lanky Texan, dropped to the ground without a word and stripped the saddle from his horse. The second, a hand at his throat, asked hoarsely, "You got any water, boss?"

Rod handed over his canteen and dug into the bag for sandwiches. "You boys be careful. Don't let anybody ride up to you like I did."

The lanky Texan glanced at Rod and showed a lopsided grin. "I signed up to drive this herd from south Texas all the way to Kansas." He took a bite of his sandwich, chewed about twice, and swallowed. "I was seventeen then and dumb as dirt. It's been a long drive. I guess I must be about forty now, but I know I'm not any smarter. Anyhow, in all this time I ain't seen one other man, not a single one, wearing a clean white shirt every day like you do. Boss, dumb as I am, I could figure who you were from a mile away."

"I beg your pardon. I meant no offense. I just wanted you men to be on your guard."

Another huge bite of half-chewed sandwich went down. The Texan grabbed the canteen from his riding partner and upended it. Bubbles rumbled in the metal canteen while a trail of water ran down both sides of his neck and darkened the front of his shirt. When the canteen finally lowered, a long sigh, a gusty belch, and a wipe across his mouth with the back of his hand seemed to replace the lopsided grin. "Us Texans don't have your slick ways, Mr. Silvana, but we don't think pulling a gun on the boss is mannerly." He pitched the canteen back to his partner and hoisted his saddle onto a fresh horse from Rod's string.

"Keep an eye peeled for Monk. Sweetbean says he's with the rustlers."

Both riders froze for a couple of seconds, staring wide-eyed at Rod. Then the Texan shrugged and stooped to tighten his saddle cinch. "That Monk ain't no Texas man. He's some kind of foreigner, probably from New York or some other godforsaken heathen place, but I never figured he'd pull a Yankee trick like that."

His silent partner said, "That bastard," handed the canteen back to Rod, mounted, and rode slowly toward the grazing cattle.

Rod checked the lead line, pulled himself back into the saddle, and headed west. Fifteen minutes later, he saw Win Mill walking toward him, leading a used-up horse. When he pulled rein and offered a sandwich, Win grabbed it and took a huge bite.

"Thirsty?"

Win shook his head and keep chewing.

"How bad are we hurt?"

Win swallowed and took a deep breath. "Not sure yet. Nobody wounded or killed that I know about." He flexed one leg and then the other. "Damn, how I hate to walk, but I already nearly killed this horse." He scrubbed his face with a rough hand and fixed icy blue eyes on Rod. "Near as I can tell, we're about five hundred to a thousand head short, but that doesn't mean much. Cattle are still joining up the bunches we're putting together. We'll know better after more daylight time."

"Is that all?"

Staring at Rod, face rigid, Win stood motionless for a long ten seconds of taut silence. Then he flexed his shoulders, rolled his head back and forth, and rubbed the back of his neck, obviously trying to loosen a creeping stiffness in a tired body. "Yes, Mr. Silvana, that's all. Nothing to cause concern. I wouldn't have you get upset about what might be a fifteen or thirty-thousand-dollar

loss, more or less. I keep forgetting you're related to my
insane brother-in-law. I keep letting you surprise me
when you act like that damn fool Milton Baynes."

"I thought you were fond of Milt."

Win took another bite of sandwich and chewed in
silence, staring off into the distance. The silence lasted
while the last of the sandwich vanished and Win switched
saddles to a fresh horse. Mounted, eyes now level with
Rod's, he said, "If I loved Milton Baynes any more than
I do, it would founder me. I couldn't bear it. My sister
married him and adores him, but that doesn't change
anything. He's still a strange pinhead with more queer
habits than a madhouse full of lunatics. The more things
go bad, the wider that irritating smirk of his gets. I guess
it runs in your family."

He stretched out and loosened the lead rope from
Rod's saddle. "Unhook those worn-out horses from the
string and take them back to the remuda. Bring some
more fresh horses as fast as you can without wearing
them out. I'll take these. I know just where to take them.
Just ride this way again. I'll have everybody watch for
you."

"Sweetbean says Monk is working with the rustlers.
Warn everybody."

Win's mouth twisted. "I don't think I can handle any
more good news. Hurry with those horses."

Rod stepped down, walked back and separated the
tired horses from the string, tied them to his own saddle,
and remounted.

"By the way, a bad run like this probably ran a lot of
meat off those critters we've been fattening up all this
time. Those we got left will probably bring us about a
dollar a head less when selling time comes. We probably
ruined half a dozen good horses last night too. Think
about all that and see if you can still grin like your crazy
cousin."

Rod nodded. "I could burst into tears, hold my breath,

turn blue, and fall over backward. Would that make you feel better?"

Win smiled and waved off the subject like he was warding off gnats. "It's your money, mostly. Oh, another thing—Milt rode off to Ellsworth. It's farther west than Abilene, and I bet we'll run into less trouble getting there, so I'm pointing the herd that direction. Milt figures Cowan will do the same thing for the same reason. Cowan should be there by now and has probably already sold his cattle. Milt said he'd get Cowan and his home crew to pass the word to all the buyers to watch out for anybody trying to sell our stock. If I know Caleb Cowan, anybody caught doing that is in for gunpowder trouble."

Win rode away at a steady lope without waiting for an answer, and Rod relaxed a minute to watch him. When he'd asked Win, "Is that all?" he'd only meant to enquire if the man had anything more to report. He hadn't meant to imply the night's losses were insignificant. Win's reaction showed how heavily the strain bore down on him. The trail boss probably hadn't had a full night's sleep for weeks. Rod turned back toward the sun and put his horse to an easy trot that he planned to slow frequently to a walk. Any faster and the tired horses behind him would probably topple over.

NINETEEN

FIVE DAYS LATER, Milton Baynes reappeared. He strolled casually into the firelight from the surrounding darkness with his coffee cup in hand. He handed the tin cup to Atha and pulled one of Rod's camp chairs closer to the table, seated himself, and glanced back at Atha, still standing with his cup dangling from her hand.

"You've taken on the job of taking care of this slick gambler. I'm his cousin, so you got to look out for me too. We're a close family."

When Atha smiled and turned away, Milt turned to Rod. "I see you've moved about twenty miles since I left. Mighty slow progress for five or six days. You must have had a tough time getting the herd back together."

To Milton Baynes, the difference between an absence of five minutes or one of five days meant little. He took up conversations like he'd only stepped away long enough to unsaddle his horse. Rod decided he had no choice but to do the same. "Every man and just about every horse is down to skin and bones. Win figures we

199

lost about five hundred head. He says we're lucky as sin."

"Well, we may get some of them back. I've been to Ellsworth."

"Win told me you decided to ride ahead."

"Caleb Cowan's already sold my herd, so I'm rich as an Egyptian pharaoh. When I told him about all this excitement, he sent riders to meet the other herds coming north to tell them to keep an eye out for your stock. If they see any of them, they'll gather them up with their own and sell them for you. Cowan opened a bank account for them to put the money into for you. Honest men, these Texas cowmen, mostly. In fact, that's the most surprising thing about them. He also sent warning to all the buyers in Ellsworth and Abilene to be on the lookout for your stuff. Anybody trying to sell any of them without declaring them to be yours is going to have to do some work covering the brands."

"Great news! Have you told Win yet?"

"Don't have to. Win's a cattleman. He knew what I was about without needing to be told."

"Ouch. I think I just got insulted."

"No, Cousin Rod, just instructed. Cattlemen help each other in all kinds of ways. Picking up strays and putting them back on the right pasture goes on all the time."

Milt leaped to his feet, whipped off his hat, and bowed when Atha returned and put his coffee down in front of him. Quick as a striking rattler, he grabbed her hand and made a wet smacking noise over it. "Oh, thank you, ma'am, thank you. I'm forever grateful for any kindness."

While Atha stood frozen in wide-eyed surprise, Milt dropped into his chair, slapped his hat back on, took a sip of coffee, and leaned forward toward Rod to speak quietly. "She's a little slow, but she obeys orders real good, and she takes teasing and joking with wonderful good humor. I always admired those traits in a woman. I think she'll fit into the family just fine, Rod."

"Mr. Baynes, what on earth are you talking about?" Atha now stood with both hands raised to her mouth, the picture of alarm or astonishment, Rod couldn't tell which.

Milt sat motionless, eyes fixed on Rod. "You haven't asked her yet?"

Rod kept his voice level. "This is outrageous. What do you think you're doing?"

With his typical effortless movement, Milt came to his feet and held a chair invitingly for Atha. "Miss Banks, will you take a seat, please?" She stood undecided for a second, then accepted the invitation.

Seated again, Milt spoke with an edge of irritation. "You two haven't made any progress in all this time? Well, I never expected that."

"Progress?" Rod lifted a brow.

"This is the situation." Milt leaned forward like a conspirator, and Rod, drawn forward in spite of himself, saw Atha do the same.

"My daddy went and married Rosalinda Ozuna Fitzpatrick."

"Our cousin?"

"Yeah, Rod, she's one of my mama's distant cousins, so maybe she's an aunt or something. She's not a real cousin like you and me. First and second cousins I can calculate, but after that I get confused."

"I'm happy for him, Milt, but what—"

Milt lifted a hand. "Pay attention. Pa and his new wife are already in Ellsworth, living in high style. They've reserved a bunch of rooms in the McCoy, a brand new fancy hotel the likes of which you never saw outside New Orleans. My wife's coming up from Texas, Ward and his wife are coming in from California, and Luke and his wife are on the way from Wyoming. While we've been on this drive, Pa called all the Baynes clan together to meet his new wife. Since I was out of touch while doing this wonderful vacation ride, Pa got everybody to come meet me when I get to Ellsworth."

"Wonderful, Milt, but I don't see—"

Milt's hand rose again. "Just hush up and let me tell it. Now, when Pa told me about all this, I was about to jump and holler with the joy of it. I just naturally wanted to come up with some good news, too, just to have something to add to the pot, don't you see. Anyhow, I told Pa about you and Miss Banks calf-eyeing each other and having long serious talks most every evening. Everybody on this drive's been watching you two spooning and getting a big kick out of it. The tight part is, sometimes my pa kind of hears better than I can talk, so maybe he heard more than I said. He up and sent a telegram to your pa, Rod, saying he'd better hustle up to Kansas if he wanted to see you get married."

"Milt, this is absolutely atrocious."

Atha sounded a little breathless. "My goodness."

Rod added, "It's unbelievable."

"I beg your pardon. Why unbelievable?" Atha's tone changed abruptly.

"You're right, Miss Banks. Nothing unbelievable about it. Pa believed it without even being told, not exactly." Milt now spoke firmly. "You two got to get married soon's we get to Ellsworth or my goose is cooked, guts, feathers, and all. Everybody will be horribly embarrassed, and they'll all blame me. I'll never live it down."

Atha came to her feet and spoke with quiet menace, eyes fixed on Rod. "Why do you find it unbelievable, Mr. Silvana?"

Rod thought fast. The conversation had taken a dangerous turn faster than the crack of a whip. "Please, Miss Banks, I meant no offense. You're a lovely woman. I can't believe anyone would think you could be interested in such as me."

Milt evidently caught the ominous turn in the conversation too. He lifted a hand, palm up, toward Atha. "Good point, Miss Banks. No argument there. He's spoiled rotten, set in his strange ways, got an uppity attitude, accustomed to being waited on hand and foot, and that's not the worst of it. He's not nearly as good looking as the men on my side of the family."

Atha turned on Milt, voice icy. "How dare you. Mr. Silvana is a fine figure of a man."

"Although spoiled, strange, and uppity," Rod said sadly as if completing her remark for her.

She turned back to face Rod and shocked him with a smile. "Few men avoid those faults. None I've ever met."

"Ow!" Milt leaped to his feet and spun around twice in a teetering dance. "She shot at you, but she got me too. I'm going off to hide and lick my wounds. Y'all be kind to one another." He vanished in seconds, limping pitifully and groaning.

"He's the funniest man I've ever met. He's like a little boy in a man's body. Everything is a big joke to him." Atha sounded like she wanted to burst out laughing.

"He has his serious moments, Miss Banks."

"Yes, I've heard the men talk about him. They say he's a deadly enemy if crossed."

"I suppose so. Now, about this embarrassing problem, Miss Banks."

"Yes?"

"Won't you please take a seat?"

She sat down and regarded him with a slight smile.

"I guess it has become obvious to everyone I have come to hold you in the highest regard."

She looked calmly into his eyes, her smile unchanged. "Thank you."

"In fact, Miss Banks, I've come to have the strongest affection for you."

"Strong affection?"

"I love you."

She remained motionless, seemed to be waiting.

Rod understood her patient stillness, knew he had to take the next step. "Milt's idea seems to me to have great merit. I hope you'll consider it, Miss Banks."

"What idea?"

He took a deep breath and plunged on. "I wish you would consider marrying me when we arrive in Ellsworth."

"Very well."

"Pardon me?"

"I'll consider it."

"Is that all?"

"That's all you asked me to do, isn't it?"

"That was not my intention. I hoped to get a more enlightening answer."

"Then you must ask a more enlightening question."

"Of course. I see that now. Will you marry me?"

"Of course."

"What's that?"

"I said, 'Of course.' "

"That means yes? You said yes?"

"Yes, I did."

"Of course."

She tittered, and he couldn't hold back a laugh. "I didn't mean to say that. It popped out and sounded horribly gauche. I meant to say I'm honored and happy and . . . things like that."

"Of course."

They sat smiling at each other for a moment before he said, "I feared you'd say no or I would have asked you long ago."

"Why? I've been after you since the moment I first saw you. I've been in love with you a long time."

"You have?"

"Of course."

"I must begin to prepare you for my father. He can be a frightening person at first."

"I'm ready for that."

"Lukie's been talking again?"

"Of course."

"I'm getting tired of that."

She smothered another burst of laughter. "All right."

After a short silence, she sighed.

"What's wrong?"

"The real question is whether you are prepared for your father."

"I beg your pardon?"

"Are you sure he'll be satisfied with me? I have no fortune, no family connections, nothing at all."

"Miss Banks, this isn't a business transaction. I'm not interested in your wealth."

"What, then?"

"Why, ah, I am taken by your good humor, your industrious energy, your kindness. You have every feminine virtue, it seems to me."

Again she lapsed into almost perfect stillness, and Rod felt increasingly uncomfortable as the hush seemed to form a tense shadow between them.

"You seem suddenly cool, Miss Banks. Have I offended? You seem so quiet and sit so still."

"You dare to call me cool? I'm sitting here wondering if you'll ever drop your suffocating formality. Will you ever be at ease enough to call me Atha, even when we are alone? I'm sitting here wondering if I must spring across this table at you, or if you'll get up all by yourself and come over here and kiss me."

He came to his feet, and she rose to welcome him, lifting her lips to meet his.

TWENTY

ANOTHER WEEK PASSED with no further trouble, and the first buyer met them about ten miles south of Ellsworth. Accompanied by three of his own men and Win Mill, the buyer rode a methodical circuit around the slow-moving herd. When the group rode up to Rod, the buyer extended a hand without dismounting. "Burl Tewks. Your animals are in fine flesh, Mr. Silvana. Mr. Mill here says you have three thousand in the herd with several hundred of them belonging to him. No need for us to waste time dickering. I'll pay twenty-five dollars a head. I pay in gold."

Milton Baynes had brought word from Caleb Cowan that the market was good, not to take less than thirty. Rod said, "Thirty a head in gold and you bought a herd."

Tewks didn't blink. "I heard you boys met trouble and Cowan took an interest. He's got riders all over the place looking for your strays, so he must have sent a rider ahead of me. All right, thirty dollars a head in gold. Done. I pay on delivery at the rail head in Ellsworth.

Your boys hold the herd and help load them on railcars.
I accept your count, but my boys will verify the tally at
the loading. No offense intended, but at this price I can't
afford to be short even a few."

Rod turned to Win Mill. At Mill's nod, he faced Tewks
again and stuck out a hand. Another brief handshake
sealed the bargain.

"Want me to leave a couple of my men to steer you in?
Or I can have them meet you a couple of miles out of
town tomorrow if you like."

"Please yourself."

"We'll see you tomorrow then. We could use a bite to
eat if you got it to spare."

Rod nodded and turned his horse toward the chuck
wagon. Tewks and his men ate a hurried meal, said a
quick thank you, and swung back into saddles.

Win pointed a hard grin toward Rod. "Tewks said
Cowan warned all the buyers we'd had trouble and might
show hard feelings toward strange riders. You never saw
a man approach so careful. I think he half expected us to
shoot on sight."

"He wasted no time or words. That's certain. He must
not have spent thirty minutes getting his men fed and
headed back toward town."

Win chuckled. "Yeah, well, that damn Milt shook him
up. He showed up behind Tewks and his men just before
they got within hailing distance. Just popped out of
the ground like Milt does sometimes, riding with his rifle
unshucked and propped on one hip. Soon as Tewks came
up to me and showed himself friendly, Milt turned his
horse and rode off. Never came close enough to say
howdy or go to hell. You know how Milt is. He's out
there somewhere right now laughing his ass off. Took me
a long time to get used to Milt's idea of fun."

Rod had had no idea how quickly and efficiently a
herd of trail-broken cattle could be loaded onto railcars.
A whirlwind of heat, dust, bellowing bedlam, and the last

steer departed. Burl Tewks had his own cowpunchers, men hired to ride the cars with the cattle, using poles to "punch" cattle back to their feet should any fall or lie down on the railcars. A downed steer could too easily be stomped to death by the others.

He stood, staring at the last departing line of cars, and felt a dull sense of fatigue mixed with a spark of joy. He licked dust from his lips and spat with a grimace. If he had a choice between another cattle drive and a prison sentence, he might well prefer prison.

"Your daddy's coming in on the next train. I just picked up his telegram from the hotel desk."

Rod turned to meet Lukie's solemn gaze. "When's the next train?"

"Two hours."

Rod turned and started toward the hotel at a fast walk. Lukie fell in beside him. "Got you a tub ordered before I left the desk. I'll lay out a suit. You got plenty of time."

By the time Rod got himself bathed and dressed, Lukie had hired a rig. "Never dawned a day when Rodrigo Silvana carried his own bags down the street."

"Thanks, Lukie."

"He isn't going to be happy."

"Why not? We made the profit he expected. We almost did, anyway."

"Never mind that, Rod. I'm talking about Atha."

"When he meets her, he'll like her."

A stony silence gave Lukie's opinion better than anything he could have said. It lasted until they sat beside the depot, watching the train pull to a stop. Rod stepped down to go welcome his father, and Lukie said, "Hold your temper."

After a dignified greeting at the train depot and a short ride to the luxurious McCoy Hotel, Rodrigo Silvana settled himself into a chair, surveyed his room briefly, and pointed to one of his steamer trunks. "Brandy. Three glasses." He pulled a key ring from a vest pocket and tossed it to Lukie.

Lukie leaped to open the trunk. As soon as he had the lid open, he turned to return the key ring to Rodrigo. Moving with the smooth speed of the trained servant familiar with his master's belongings, he pulled a traveling case from an interior drawer, flipped it open, and set three brandy snifters in a row on a side table. He pulled a white linen napkin from the case and polished each snifter with a few deft strokes. Another swift motion brought out a bottle. A splash of brandy left an amber stain at the bottom of each of the snifters before Lukie's gaze rose to meet Rodrigo's.

The elder Silvana made a slight motion and Lukie doubled the portions in each snifter. When Lukie looked up again, he received a nod. Swiftly, he placed a glass beside the father, one beside the son, and then stood beside the third, eyes fixed on Rodrigo.

"Pick that up."

Lukie picked up the third glass.

"Sit."

Rod eased himself into the chair facing his father.

"You too."

Lukie stiffened, coming even more rigidly erect, and glanced at Rod. Rod made no move, careful to control his expression. Lukie, trained from earliest childhood never to sit in the presence of the elder Silvana, didn't move. He held the brandy snifter in front of himself, the posture of a man looking for someone to hand it to.

"Sit down, Lukie."

He sat on the edge of a chair against the wall.

Rodrigo pointed to a spot beside his son. "Pull your chair over here, Lukie. Put it right there."

When Lukie perched himself rigidly on the chair in the designated spot, Rodrigo said, "You may now explain in more detail, son, what these cryptic telegrams I've received mean."

"We sold the cattle, sir."

"Good."

"The money is on deposit in the bank here."

"Good."

"We lost some cattle, but we doubled your investment."

"Good."

The pause in the conversation lengthened while the elder Silvana sat motionless, eyes fixed on Rod. The silence lasted long enough to convey ominous signals.

The next words spoken, "Is that all, son?" came in the quiet tone Rod had associated all his life with controlled anger from his father.

"We hired a young man along the way. He has a sister. I didn't feel we should leave her behind all alone. They have no other family." Rod took a deep breath. "Along the trail, I fell in love with the girl. I asked her to marry me. She said yes."

Again that awful silence fell, and Rod felt tension building inside him until he feared his bones might creak.

Rodrigo swirled his brandy in the snifter, warming the spirit with a cupped hand under the globe, inhaled softly to enjoy the bouquet, and took a sip.

"You hired a vagrant, penniless, orphan boy out on the prairie?"

"Yes, sir."

"You picked up a little waif sister of his and took her several hundred miles on a cattle drive with a crew of rough, common laborers?"

"Yes, sir."

"You fell in love with this little waif and asked her to marry you?"

"Yes, sir."

"And she said yes?"

"Yes, sir."

"And it never occurred to you that I might not approve."

"It occurred to me, sir."

"But that didn't stop you."

"No, sir."

Rodrigo broke the fixed eye contact with his son to glance at Lukie. "Drink your brandy, you young fool. I've got eyes in my head. You've been drinking with my son for years."

Lukie, his expression precisely that of a man expecting to be shot, took a tiny sip.

Rodrigo's hard gaze centered again on his son. "Holds his liquor better than you, I suppose?"

"Yes, sir. I think he does."

Again the stony eyes shifted to Lukie. "Your young woman's father was injured on the job, so her family fell on hard times. I felt it necessary to intervene until you could return and look after things."

Lukie came to his feet. "You gave them money? God bless you, sir. I'll repay every cent, with interest."

"I do not give money away. That is a vice that has never afflicted me. I offered her employment in my household until you return or her father recovers. She's a bright and energetic young woman who earns her wages. There is no debt to be paid."

Lukie stood very still for a moment, obviously inde-cisive, before he sank back down into his chair. Rod caught his eye and dropped one eyelid a fraction of an inch. Best for both of them to say nothing. To ask how his father knew about Lukie's love interest would be considered unbearably indelicate.

"Now, about this orphan you've become enamored with."

"Father, I believe you'll find her very attractive. I suggest you meet her before you make any decisions."

"I'm afraid that my meeting her will mean little or nothing." Rodrigo rose and bent over his open trunk. When he straightened, he held an obviously heavy bronze chest about a foot square and four inches deep. He glanced at Lukie. "Pull a chair for my son over beside this table."

He pulled his key ring from his vest pocket again and

unlocked the metal box. "Inside, you will find a stack of four trays. Each tray contains a collection of rings, each tagged with a number. Held to the inside of the top of the box by a leather strap is a small book giving a description and the history of each ring, identified by its number. Some of those jewels have been in our family since the Middle Ages. You come from an old and honorable family. If you choose to bring this young woman into our family, she should know what that means, and you should select which of these heirlooms you want to serve as the wedding ring she will wear the rest of her life."

"Does this mean you don't object, Father?"

"It means that it's too late for that, Son. You've asked, and she has answered. The time for objections has passed. You've given your word."

Rod stepped close and embraced his rigid father, and he felt a shock of surprise to find himself surrounded by his father's arms. Slowly they drew apart, and Rod saw moisture in his father's eyes. But Rodrigo blinked, turned away, and spoke in his customary arid tone of authority. "Brandy."

Lukie, trying desperately to control a smile, sprang for the bottle.

TWENTY-ONE

ROD STOOD IN the McCoy Hotel parlor and smiled at the assembled group. A whole bunch of his family he hadn't seen for years stood smiling back at him.

Rodrigo Silvana, wearing an unfamiliar relaxed and happy expression, stood chatting with his closest friend, the towering Darnell Baynes, and his statuesque wife Rosalinda. Darnell's equally tall and powerfully built first son, Luke, sat nearby, with his spectacular blond wife Helen resting her hand on his arm in her possessive way. Milton, amazingly well-behaved in the presence of his feisty wife, Cris, with hair like a halo of flame, smirked in secret amusement at everything around him. Rod hardly recognized him in his spotless, tailored town garb. Ward, dressed in his California Spanish mode, hovered around his petite wife, Kit, as if she were made of delicate porcelain.

Lukie edged up beside him and whispered, "You remember that outlaw you shot when they attacked the herd?"

"Sure, what brought that to your mind about five minutes before I get married?"

"Well, I was talking to your daddy about that night. He's been curious but too proud to ask you how it all went. You know how he likes the details. Anyway, he said I ought to tell you."

"Tell me what?"

"You remember that fat gambler you caught cheating on the boat coming to Texas?"

"Sure. Why?"

"He was the one you shot out on the prairie. One and the same."

"Coincidence, don't you think, Lukie?"

"Guess so. Next time, shoot a skinny one if you want me to bury him. That was a big job."

"Poor baby."

"Here comes the preacher, boss."

"You lose the ring yet, best man?"

"Don't you worry none. I got the ring, and I'm right behind you. If you start to fall, I'll hold you up. You don't suppose Atha got smart and ran off, do you?"

The barroom pianist started the wedding march, and Atha stepped into view at the top of the stairs leading into the hotel ballroom. She began her stately descent, timing her movements to the music, a slim vision in a cloud of white. Rod could never explain what drew his attention to his father at that moment, but their eyes met.

Rodrigo Vasquez Allesandro Castillo y Silvana, stiffly erect, face set in habitually haughty, unsmiling lines, stared directly into his son's eyes . . . and winked.